Hiya!

I was SO excited to be asked to write a mini book for World Book Day . . . whoa! I'm in the middle of writing a series called the Chocolate Box Girls right now, so I thought it would be fun to write a story about one of the characters from the series.

Lots of readers fell for cool surf-boy Shay Fletcher from my book *Cherry Crush* . . . so, by popular demand, here is a brand-new story from his viewpoint!

Shay's life is ticking over pretty well; he has a cute girlfriend, good friends, a talent for writing songs and playing guitar. And then it all falls apart. Have *you* ever messed up big time? If so, I think you'll like Shay's story. Will he get a happy ending? You'll have to read on and see . . .

Keep reading, keep smiling – and follow your dreams!

Cathy Cassidy xxx

Cathy Cassidy

Bitter Sweet

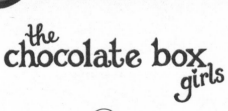

the chocolate box girls

PUFFIN

PUFFIN BOOKS

Published by the Penguin Group
Penguin Books Ltd, 80 Strand, London WC2R 0RL, England
Penguin Group (USA) Inc., 375 Hudson Street, New York, New York 10014, USA
Penguin Group (Canada), 90 Eglinton Avenue East, Suite 700, Toronto, Ontario, Canada M4P 2Y3
(a division of Pearson Penguin Canada Inc.)
Penguin Ireland, 25 St Stephen's Green, Dublin 2, Ireland (a division of Penguin Books Ltd)
Penguin Group (Australia), 707 Collins Street, Melbourne, Victoria 3008, Australia
(a division of Pearson Australia Group Pty Ltd)
Penguin Books India Pvt Ltd, 11 Community Centre, Panchsheel Park, New Delhi – 110 017, India
Penguin Group (NZ), 67 Apollo Drive, Rosedale, Auckland 0632, New Zealand
(a division of Pearson New Zealand Ltd)
Penguin Books (South Africa) (Pty) Ltd, Block D, Rosebank Office Park, 181 Jan Smuts Avenue,
Parktown North, Gauteng 2193, South Africa

Penguin Books Ltd, Registered Offices: 80 Strand, London WC2R 0RL, England

puffinbooks.com

First published 2013
001

Text copyright © Cathy Cassidy, 2013
All rights reserved

The moral right of the author have been asserted

Set in Baskerville MT
Printed in Great Britain by Clays Ltd, St Ives plc

British Library Cataloguing in Publication Data
A CIP catalogue record for this book is available from the British Library

ISBN: 978-0-141-34724-0

www.greenpenguin.co.uk

Penguin Books is committed to a sustainable
future for our business, our readers and our
planet. This book is made from paper certified
by the Forest Stewardship Council.

ALWAYS LEARNING   PEARSON

Bitter Sweet

A seagull's call cuts through the misty morning
Sunlight hasn't touched the blankets yet . . .
I hear your voice whisper in my waking dream,
And tell myself you're here, and I forget –
How yesterday your smiling eyes they left me;
How yesterday your heart it turned away;
Last night I dreamt of cherry-blossom trees, but now
Comes the bittersweet reality of day . . .

Cherry-blossom sweet, bitter taste of pain
Say you won't forget me, love me still.
Cherry-blossom sweet, bitter taste of pain
Give me one more chance . . . be mine again.

I sit down by the waterfront, it's evening.
The tide comes washing in over my feet.
It's so like you in every move it makes . . .
It rushed forward to me then, but now retreats.
If there's one thing I know about the ocean
The same thing I can hope for your heart.
The sea will always find its way back to the shore . . .
Can we both find our way back to the start?

Cherry-blossom sweet, bitter taste of pain
Say you won't forget me, love me still.
Cherry-blossom sweet, bitter taste of pain
Give me one more chance . . . be mine again.

1

Sometimes, your life can change in a moment and you might not even know it.

You could be sitting on a beach at sunset with a bunch of friends, playing guitar and singing while people laugh and chat and toast marshmallows, a party going on all around you. You might not notice the tall bearded guy listening intently, or know that he has the power to turn everything upside down for you. Doors could open, opportunities could unfold. Fame and fortune could hook you in, and nothing would ever be the same again.

My friend Finch jabbed me in the ribs, grinning.

'See that guy with the beard, over there?' he asked. 'He's a friend of Mum's, from back home in London. She told him about your playing, and he said he'd come down one weekend and listen. He's called Curtis Rawlins. You should say hello.'

'Yeah?' I echoed, peering into the twilight. 'You think?'

Things had been crazy lately – a TV company was making a film in the village, and Finch's mum Nikki was the producer. She and Finch had been staying with my girlfriend's family for the summer, but the film was all wrapped up now. Nikki and Finch were ready to head back to London – the beach party was a kind of goodbye get-together.

Nikki had heard me play a few times over the holidays, though I'd never thought anything of it. The guy with Nikki looked like your typical film-crew type, youngish and London-cool with a goatee beard and a red trilby hat. I lifted a hand to wave at the two of them, and they grinned back.

'Curtis is a talent scout for a record company,' Finch said into my ear. 'Wrecked Rekords . . . you've heard of them, right?'

I blinked. Everyone has heard of Wrecked Rekords – some of my favourite bands are signed to them.

'Hang on, Finch,' I frowned. 'Did you just say . . .'

'Curtis is a talent scout, yeah,' he repeated.

'Wow. But no, the other bit . . .'

'Right. The bit about Mum telling him about your playing?' Finch checked. 'Yeah. She sent him a copy of that CD you made for me, and a link to your online stuff, and he liked it and decided to come down and meet you. He's been listening to you for the last hour. So . . . are you going to say hi?'

He nudged me forward.

'Hey, Nikki, Curtis,' I said politely.

2

The beardy guy grinned and shook my hand, and up close I could see he had about a dozen piercings in one ear. 'Shay, isn't it?' he said. 'Nice playing. And they're all your own songs?'

I said that they were, and Curtis asked if I'd ever recorded anything or if I might like to. Wrecked Rekords were always on the lookout for new talent. According to Curtis, I was just the kind of thing they were looking for.

'Seriously?' I remember saying. 'Me?'

Curtis was serious.

It could have been that easy, I swear. I could have had a recording contract right there and then, with a cool London label. Curtis said he thought I had something special – raw talent, awesome songs, an offbeat kind of charm. Plus, I was young and keen and had the right look.

Me. Really. He said I could have a career, a future. They'd put down a few tracks, arrange some showcase gigs, get media coverage.

'You could be big,' Curtis told me. 'That indie-ballad vibe, the bittersweet songs, the surf-boy looks . . . it's unique. They're going to love you!'

My life could have changed in that moment, but . . .

Well, it didn't. Just my luck.

Thing is, I am fifteen. I am still at school, and Curtis said that was no problem at all, but that obviously my parents would have to be on board with the whole thing.

'Don't worry,' he told me. 'I'll talk to them, explain it all. Trust me!'

That's when I knew I was doomed. My parents were never going to listen to a bloke with a goatee beard and piercings and a red trilby hat, talking about bittersweet songs with a surf-boy twist. It just wouldn't happen.

'I'm heading back to London tomorrow, but I'll call in before I go,' Curtis said. 'When would be a good time?'

'We work Sundays,' I told him. 'My dad runs the sailing centre in the village, and Sunday is one of our busiest days . . .'

'I'll definitely need to speak to him,' Curtis said.

I sighed. 'Well . . . our bookings don't start until eleven on weekends, so if you called in around ten Dad should still be home . . .'

'Cool,' Curtis grinned.

But it wasn't cool at all, and I wasn't the only one who thought so.

'D'you think you'd better tell your dad first?' my girlfriend Cherry said. 'Just mention it, set the scene a bit. So it doesn't come as too much of a shock?'

'Maybe,' I said.

'I think you should,' she persisted. 'You know what he's like. A bit cynical? You have to give him time to get used to the idea, prepare him a bit, or else he'll never even let Curtis over the doorstep!'

I looked up at the moon, a crescent of silver in the dark September sky. I was looking for inspiration, ideas, but the moon just blinked back at me, impassive.

'I'll tell him first thing tomorrow,' I promised Cherry.

Let's just say it didn't go too well.

I spilled the beans over breakfast – Dad's favourite scrambled-egg feast. I even made him a banana smoothie with cinnamon sprinkles, but it was no use. He said no – actually, he yelled it, and there was a lot of swearing mixed in there too, so I knew he wasn't about to change his mind. I texted Cherry to tell her, and she rang back right away, telling me not to give up.

'Give him time to mull it over,' she insisted. 'You might be surprised.'

'Doubt it,' I huffed. 'He won't listen . . . He hates the whole idea. Hopeless.'

'Nikki and Curtis can explain things better, though,' Cherry pointed out. 'The whole thing will have more weight, more gravity, coming from them. You've done the groundwork . . . relax, Shay. They'll soon talk your dad round.'

Ha. Pigs might fly.

*

Now, half an hour later, I'm sitting on my bedroom window sill wishing I had never heard of Curtis Rawlins. I don't think Dad has calmed down and started to accept the idea of me getting a record deal, not from the dark, brooding look on his face or the way he is stomping around the kitchen. Mum and Ben have made themselves scarce and headed down to the sailing centre to set up.

'Not looking good, little brother,' Ben said as he left. 'Sorry.'

I'm sorry too. I press my face against the bedroom window, watching the path, hoping to spot Curtis coming and head him off before Dad gets hold of him. Things could get messy. In the end, I am not fast enough – Dad whips the door open just as Curtis and Nikki are striding up the path, their faces bright with opportunity and hope.

'Whatever you want from us, it's not happening,' Dad is roaring even before I can get down into the hallway. 'I know your sort. Whatever kind of deal you are offering, forget it – my son wants nothing to do with you!'

'Please, Mr Fletcher,' Finch's mum says. 'Hear us out. I can assure you that Curtis is making a very genuine offer here –'

'Not interested,' Dad snaps, and my heart sinks. He is not going to budge, not even for a film producer and a London record company talent scout. Especially not for them.

'I'm not sure if you realize,' Curtis says, 'but Shay here could really make his mark in the music business. Wrecked Rekords would nurture him, develop him, perfect the product and polish up his performance skills . . .'

'I don't think so,' Dad says.

'But, Mr Fletcher – Shay's got it all. Looks, skill, a unique style . . .'

Dad's eyes skim over Curtis with his goatee beard and piercings and red trilby hat. He grits his teeth, struggling not to share his opinion of the talent scout's own unique style.

'Nothing doing,' Dad repeats firmly. 'The music business is all drink and drugs and debauchery. It's corrupt, that's what it is. No son of mine is going in for all that malarky!'

'It doesn't have to be like that,' Nikki argues. 'You could manage him, make sure he was looked after. Shay has a talent. You wouldn't want him to waste that, Mr Fletcher, would you?'

'Talent?' Dad snorts. 'When has talent ever been enough? You've been watching too much *X-Factor*. Listen, because I don't think you heard me the first time. Over. My. Dead. Body. Clear enough for you?'

I cringe. How can he be so rude, so aggressive? I bite my lip and roll my eyes, and hope that Nikki and Curtis know how mortified I am feeling.

'All that showbiz nonsense,' Dad rants on. 'Ridiculous! Shay is fifteen years old. He's still at school, and I need him here at the sailing centre too. This is a family business, in case you haven't noticed. And it's real work, proper physical work, not your airy-fairy music rubbish!'

'Dad!' I cut in. 'Please? This is a once-in-a-lifetime chance! If you'd just give Nikki and Curtis a fair hearing –'

'I've listened,' he huffs. 'And I didn't like what I heard. It's a con, Shay, can't you see that? So, thanks, but . . . no thanks.'

He smiles icily and tries to shut the door, but Curtis turns back at the last minute, sticks his foot against the door frame and hands Dad his card and a sheaf of forms and leaflets.

'Think about it,' he says. 'No pressure. You know where to reach me if you change your mind.'

He steps back just in time to avoid a bunch of broken toes as Dad slams the door. The forms and leaflets go straight in the bin, of course. Much later, when the worst day of my life is finally over and Dad has gone to bed, I fish the papers out and stuff them into my rucksack, even though they are slightly crumpled and have a nasty brown stain from where a tea bag has landed on them.

I am not about to give up that easily.

2

It's not that my dad doesn't believe in talent – I think he believes in it too much. He knows that fame and fortune can be very fickle things. It's just that as far as Dad is concerned, all of the talent in our family belongs to my big brother.

Ben is a bit of a legend around here. He's brilliant at sport, football especially . . . he was playing for Bristol City FC Youth Squad by the time he was fourteen, and Southampton FC scouted him when he was sixteen, but he had an injury and things didn't work out. It wasn't majorly serious, but it was enough to wipe out Ben's chances of a premier-league football career.

Dad didn't cope too well when it all went pear-shaped. He couldn't believe you could play so well and work so hard and have it all end in nothing, and I suppose that has made him suspicious of chances and opportunities and promises of fame and fortune.

Anyhow, Ben went off to uni to study sports science and said it was the best thing he ever did. He went out every night and partied hard, doing all the stuff he hadn't done when he was younger because of training so hard, and this summer he graduated with a 2:1 degree and started working full time at the sailing centre. He works hard, but he parties hard too.

'You're only young once, Shay,' he likes to tell me. 'Take my advice – loosen up, little brother. Live a little!'

I don't take Ben's advice, though.

I haven't done that since I was five years old. Ben had made a go-cart and he told me I could be the first person to test it out. I felt like the most important boy in the world as I followed him up the hill behind our cottage.

'You have total control,' he told me. 'Just yank on the steering rope to turn left or right, or to slow down. You're so lucky I chose you to be the test driver, Shay! It's going to be epic!'

It was epic all right. I wedged myself into the driver's seat and Ben pushed me off down the hill at about a million miles an hour. Three seconds into the ride, the steering rope came off in my hands and, of course, there were no brakes. By the time I got to the bottom of the hill I was yelling like crazy. A wheel came off as I sped across the yard and crashed into the cottage wall, and I fell out of the go-cart and squashed Mum's flowers and broke my arm in two different places.

Ben was the first to reach me.

'Don't tell,' he hissed into my ear as I lay in a mangled heap beneath the lupins. 'I'll get into terrible trouble, and you wouldn't want that, would you?'

So I didn't tell, not even when Dad shouted at me for taking Ben's go-cart without permission, not even when Mum grumbled about the squashed flower beds, not even when the doctors at A & E prodded about at my broken arm and put a plaster cast on it. I cried a bit because I was only five, remember, and it hurt a LOT. But Ben told me not to make a fuss, so after a while I just bit my lip and tried to be brave.

'How did you manage to get yourself into such a mess, Shay?' Dad huffed. 'Why can't you be more like your brother?'

That's the question they've all been asking, my whole life pretty much. I wish I knew the answer, but the truth is I am not like Ben. We are chalk and cheese, day and night, sunshine and shadow.

I sigh, prising the lid off a fresh tin of paint, dipping my brush neatly and stroking the foul-smelling stuff across the upturned hull of yet another dinghy.

It's Monday evening, almost two whole days after the legendary moment that didn't change my life. Things have continued to go downhill. Finch and

Nikki headed back to London along with Curtis, and with them leaving it felt like summer was well and truly over, all the fun squeezed out of it. I will miss Finch, miss the freedom of long hot days that blur into lazy nights of music and laughter.

It's like Dad has slammed the door on all of that too.

To top it all, today school started up again. I managed to survive it, but only just – my mind switched off as the teachers began to talk about how important Year Eleven is, how hard we'll need to study to pass our GCSEs and get that golden ticket to a shining future – it is hard to get worked up about exams right now. What's the point? I will probably flunk my GCSEs and drop out of school to face a life of slavery at the sailing centre, scraping barnacles off boats and teaching little kids how to kayak.

I kept my head down and hoped that nobody was talking about what happened with Curtis, but word had definitely leaked out because at break a few kids asked if it was true I was going to be recording with Wrecked Rekords. I pretended not to know what they were talking about, but that just fuelled the rumour.

Wait till they get the whole story – the boy who was offered a record deal from Wrecked and turned it down? Yup, that's me.

I'll look like the biggest loser in the universe.

It is a relief to be back here, away from the gossip, away from the sad glances Cherry keeps shooting me when she thinks I'm not looking. Nobody likes to be pitied, right?

I dip my brush again and focus on painting.

So, yeah . . . my brother, the legend.

When I was seven, Ben scored three goals in the final match of the Under Thirteens' Somerset football league and got his picture in the paper holding a shiny silver cup up in the air. Dad put up a shelf in the bedroom we shared to display the trophy, and when that shelf got crowded he put up another. When that one was full, Dad cleared my shelves so that Ben could use them too. It's not like I was going to win any trophies – that sporty, competitive gene must have skipped me completely.

'Shay Fletcher?' a whole bunch of teachers have said over the years, usually out on the sports field. 'Ben's little brother? Goodness, you don't take after him, do you?'

Ben is popular with the girls, of course. They look at his blond hair and his athletic build and his skin tanned golden from working outside at the sailing centre, and they swoon. There are always little gangs of them cheering him on from the sidelines at any given football match. All he has to do is smile and reel them in. He has a girlfriend from uni, but she lives miles away in Sheffield, and that's probably a good thing. At least she's not around to watch my brother flirting with every female within a fifty-mile radius.

I do not have an athletic build or a budding career in football, but I have the wheat-blond hair and the sea-green eyes and the tan. It took me a while to suss that not every girl who asked me if I was Ben Fletcher's little brother was angling for his mobile number. Some of them were actually interested in ME.

'Way to go, little brother,' Ben laughed, when I started dating Honey Tanberry back in Year Nine. I had my brother's approval at last.

I probably wouldn't have dated Honey for half as long as I did if it hadn't been for that. She was hard work – behind the party-girl facade, she was all anger and hurt and hopelessness. Neither of us got along with our families, and for a while that kept us together. I thought I could make her happy, but it turns out I was wrong about that, and after a while her drama-queen stuff started to get to me a bit.

I couldn't see why Honey lashed out against her mum, why she hated her new stepdad. They both seemed pretty cool to me, but when I said that she called me a traitor. After a while I started to feel like I was just some kind of cool accessory she liked to have in tow, a boy with a guitar who was good for her image.

The two of us were just marking time, hanging out together until something better came along . . . at least, that's what I thought.

It ended badly, of course.

I met Cherry, and that was it – *ka-boom*, it blew everything I'd felt for Honey right out of the water. Honey would never have forgiven me anyhow for ditching her for someone new, but I guess I didn't make it easy for her. As far as she was concerned, I'd chosen the worst possible girl to fall for. I might as well have stabbed her through the heart, she raged at me – that was how cruel, how callous I'd been. It was bad, I admit – about as bad as it was possible to get.

Cherry was her new stepsister.

The whole thing was a nightmare, a mess, a massacre.

Honey screamed and yelled and threw stuff at me, and even now, more than a year on, she looks at me with such coldness I can feel icicles form in my hair, frost chilling my skin. Like I said, it's a nightmare.

I finish painting the last dinghy, press the lid down on the paint and walk across to the storeroom to clean the brush. Over the last few years, I have turned the storeroom into a kind of den – there's an ancient, paint-spattered sofa and a kettle to boil water for a pot noodle or a hot chocolate. It's a good place to curl up with my guitar, a place to think and dream and write songs in the evening without Dad breathing down my neck.

There are plenty of pot noodles on the shelf and half a bar of Dairy Milk left over from the weekend. I reckon I've missed supper already, and it's not like I'll be missing much if I stay out another hour or two. Just the odd cutting remark from Dad, a few frosty silences, the occasional pitying glance from Mum or Ben.

It's almost sunset, and the September sky is streaked with pink and gold, but the storeroom is dark and shadowy as I step inside. I don't notice her at first, and when I do I just about jump out of my skin.

Honey is perched on the worktop in the corner, half hidden in the shadows, her long legs swinging, her jaw-length blonde hair rumpled. Her eyeliner is smudged and the lashes that fringe her wide blue eyes are damp, as if she's been crying.

'Shay?' she says, her voice small, uncertain. 'I need your help. I'm in trouble – big trouble.'

3

Honey is no stranger to trouble, of course. It's her talent, her skill. If there was an exam in it she would get an A* without even trying . . . she's a natural.

I got used to mopping up the fallout, back when we were together; Honey messing up, me sorting things out – it was just what we did. Still, I cannot for the life of me figure out what Honey is doing here now.

'OK,' I prompt, one eyebrow raised. 'What is it this time? Fire, flood, plague of frogs? Or have you just broken a fingernail?'

Harsh, I know, but you have to remember that Honey and I are not exactly friends these days. Her lips begin to quiver and her eyes blur with tears, and right away I wish I could take the words back. What if something really serious has happened?

Honey is crying harder now, her shoulders shaking, mascara running down her cheeks in ugly black streaks. I hate it when girls cry. I never know what to do.

'Hey, hey,' I say, patting her arm awkwardly. 'It can't be that bad!'

Honey burrows her head against my neck and I panic because this clearly means that things *are* that bad, or possibly worse. Me and my big mouth. What if Honey's mum has been diagnosed with a life-threatening illness or her no-good dad has finally gone bankrupt and topped himself by jumping off the Sydney Harbour Bridge? And here's me making jokes about broken fingernails. Nice one, Shay.

Meanwhile, Honey is clutching on to my T-shirt and making a wet patch on my shoulder. I can smell her favourite vanilla and almond shampoo, the scent of peppermint from the gum she likes to chew. I put an arm round her, then withdraw it again because it all feels a bit too close for comfort. This is not good.

'Shhh, Honey,' I say gently. 'Don't cry. Why don't you tell me about it?'

We sit down side by side on the beat-up sofa, the way we used to back when we were dating, and Honey dries her eyes with a corner of my T-shirt, leaving smudges of eyeliner and glittery shadow.

'They hate me,' she announces finally, her voice a whisper. 'They really do. Just because I was a little bit late home last night . . .'

Back when I used to date Honey, her curfew was 11 p.m., earlier on a school night, but Cherry tells me that those days are gone. These days, Honey is either 'grounded' or 'ungrounded', and right now I am pretty sure it's 'grounded'. Just a few weeks ago she accidentally set fire to a stable while sharing a forbidden ciggy with one of the boys from the film crew, and her sister Summer fainted while trying to fight the flames and ended up in hospital. How did Honey handle it? By taking a handful of cash from a kitchen drawer and running away. They found her at Heathrow airport trying to buy a ticket to fly out to her dad in Australia, and the last I heard she was grounded until Christmas.

Unless I am mistaken, it is not Christmas yet.

'I stayed over with a friend, obviously,' Honey is saying. 'No big deal, right? I've done it before. And it was the last night of the school holidays – you'd think they'd give me a little bit of leeway!'

But Honey is the kind of girl who takes a little bit of leeway and turns it into a wagonload of chaos, as far as I can remember.

'So I bent the rules a little,' she goes on. 'So what? I stayed with a friend and I would have gone straight to school from there, but I accidentally slept in. It was unlucky, sure, but it's not a crime, is it? Only Mum had to go and call the school, then the police . . . you name it. Talk about overreacting!'

I frown.

'Let's get this straight,' I say. 'You stayed out all night and didn't come home in the morning, and then you skipped school too. Plus, three weeks ago you ran away from home . . . Honey, don't you think your mum had reason to panic?'

'No!' she argues. 'I didn't skip school, I just slept in! And I was perfectly fine all the time, just staying with a friend, I told you! They practically had a search party out looking for me, I swear . . . crazy. So now I am in trouble at school and if that's not bad enough, the police have been on my case, telling me I am treading a very fine line . . . what does that even mean?'

'Dunno,' I shrug.

'I'll tell you exactly what it means,' Honey says, and her eyes brim with tears again. 'It means they'll get social services involved if I land up in trouble again. Can you believe that? SOCIAL SERVICES! Like I'm some kind of problem teen or something! It's just TOTALLY unfair – I wasn't even trying to run away! It's all Mum and Paddy's fault – they want rid of me! They'd be GLAD if I was taken into care!'

Honey is sobbing again now, and I am praying for rescue because I so do not want to be here right now. I spot a clean paint rag on the arm of the sofa and hand it to Honey to wipe her eyes, but she ignores it and burrows in against my shoulder again. Loads of boys I know would love to get up close and personal with Honey

Tanberry, but I am not one of them.

Not any more.

My mobile rings, and Cherry's name and picture flash up on the screen. This is not the kind of rescue I was hoping for – I jump back from Honey as if I've been stung.

'I don't bite, you know,' she says, looking hurt.

'No. I know. It's just – well – it's Cherry.'

'Don't answer,' Honey begs. 'Not right now. Just give me five minutes, please? I know you don't think much of me, Shay, but surely I'm worth that much? For old time's sake?'

I hesitate, frowning.

'Call her back later,' Honey prompts. 'Please?'

I let my mobile ring out. I feel bad, but I am not sure how I would explain to Cherry that I am holed up in the storeroom den with my ex-girlfriend, mopping up her tears with my T-shirt. It would sound a whole lot worse than it actually is.

'Thanks, Shay,' she says in a tiny voice. 'I can talk to you – I always could. Nobody else understands. And . . . well, you don't judge me.'

I'm not sure about that.

'Look,' I tell her, exasperated. 'I can see why you're upset, Honey, but you need to calm down, get a bit of perspective. This isn't Charlotte and Paddy's fault – they must have been worried sick when you went missing!'

'I wasn't missing!' Honey sulks.

'So they knew where you were?'

'Well, no . . . but . . .'

'Honey, you were grounded,' I remind her. 'You vanished without telling anyone where you were going, and you were out all night and most of the next day. You didn't turn up at school. What were they meant to think?'

Honey hugs her knees, suddenly looking about ten years old instead of fifteen.

'How come you're always so smart?' she whispers. 'OK. So I messed up . . . but the point is, I'm in trouble. I have some sort of weird police record now for running away, and the threat of social services hanging over my head. That's really not fair. And Mum and Paddy hate me, Shay, they really do! I may as *well* be taken into care because they're threatening me with some kind of boarding-school boot camp anyhow. I mean, just shoot me now. Really. My life sucks.'

I shrug. 'You think you're the only one who's had a bad day?'

Honey gives me a sideways look. 'Yeah,' she says. 'Cherry mentioned about that whole Wrecked Rekords thing. Not to me, of course . . . your little girlfriend doesn't chat to me much, funnily enough. But . . . yeah, I heard. Bummer. Your dad's still being his usual charming self then?'

'You could say that.'

'Basically, we've both been dumped on,' Honey declares. 'You just got offered the chance of a lifetime, the chance to make your dream happen – and your dad shot the whole thing down in flames. Nice.'

The anger I have been trying to keep buried all day comes bubbling up to the surface, seeping through my veins like bitter poison. It hurts, like an ache inside, a sickness. No matter how hard I work, I know I will never be able to please my dad or make him proud; Ben seems to do all of that without even trying.

Somehow, I am always second best. The things I want, the things I am good at, never count for anything.

'My family want rid of me,' Honey is saying. 'Whether it's social services or boarding school, they don't especially care which. I might as well just run away . . . it's like they expect me to anyway.'

'They were just worried,' I echo, but Honey's eyes darken and gleam.

'We could, you know,' she whispers. 'Run away, I mean. You and me. We could jump a train up to London and lie about our age and find a flat. You could record your songs with Wrecked after all, and play gigs . . . maybe you'd be famous. And I could be a designer or something, I could make really cool dresses and have a stall in Camden, and perhaps I'd get spotted too . . .'

The tiniest spark of excitement, of possibility, runs through me before the cold water of reality extinguishes it. Running away is not about finding flats and getting famous, it's about sleeping rough and going hungry night after night, and being dragged into a scary, predatory underworld. It would not be fun or cool or daring, it would be crazy, dangerous, totally disastrous.

Besides . . . Honey and me? I don't think so. Where has that even come from?

'Forget it, Honey,' I say. 'It wouldn't work out like that.'

'It might!' she argues. 'We could show them – our families, everyone – prove we can make it without their help. They'd be sorry then! And what have we got to lose?'

'Plenty,' I tell her. 'Better to stay and grab some GCSE passes and maybe some A levels . . . that could be our passport out of here. I want to go to uni and study music. London or Leeds or Liverpool, somewhere miles from here. And you could go to art college, Honey. That used to be what you wanted, not so long ago.'

'My grades aren't so good lately,' she admits sulkily. 'And uni is still years away . . . we're only fifteen. I don't know if I can survive that long!'

'If I can, you can,' I point out. 'Besides, if you run away the police will track you down. And what then? Social services will wade in, just like you said. That's just what you *don't* want.'

'I guess . . .'

Her shoulders slump and she looks suddenly vulnerable. I've always known that underneath the stroppy, rebel-girl surface Honey Tanberry is just a kid, hurt and lost and angry because her dad went away and left her just when she needed him most.

'What is it about us that's so awful, Shay?' she asks in a small, sad voice. 'What makes us so difficult to love?'

'I don't know,' I sigh.

This time, when she leans against me and drops her head against my shoulder, I don't pull away.

 *4*

When I get on the school bus next morning, Cherry waves me over and I flop into the seat beside her. My eyes slide to the back of the bus where Honey usually holds court, but there is no sign of her. Last night I talked her out of running away to London and into sticking things out at school. I talked her into going home and at midnight I walked her along the lane to her gate. What if she didn't go home after all? What if she waited in the trees until I'd gone, then headed off into the darkness along the lane, hitching a lift to London?

Were the late night heart-to-hearts and pep talks all for nothing?

'What happened to you last night?' Cherry is asking. 'I kept calling, but no reply.'

'Sorry . . . my mobile died, and I didn't notice till this morning . . . I've left it at home on charge.'

'Oh? It seemed to be ringing . . . it didn't go to voicemail or anything . . .'

'My mobile does that sometimes,' I bluff. 'It acts kind of weird when the battery's flat.'

The lie drips too easily off my tongue, but it's

safer than the truth. I am not sure how Cherry would feel if she knew I'd sat up till midnight in the storeroom den with Honey, telling her every single thing about Curtis and Dad and how let down I felt. I don't think she'd understand – I'm not even sure I do.

'No worries,' Cherry says. 'I guessed it would be something like that – I know you wouldn't just ignore me. I just wanted to make sure you were OK – thought you might be feeling low.'

'I'm fine,' I tell her. 'Or I will be, anyhow. I just don't want to be around Dad right now – I stayed late at the sailing centre last night, painting boats. It was OK . . . boring, I guess, but after a while your head just switches off and the job takes over. Then I holed up in the den and played guitar. I totally lost track of the time . . . didn't get to bed till late.'

'Aw, I bet,' Cherry sighs. 'Poor Shay. You must be so hacked off with your dad – all your dreams shattered before they even got off the ground.'

'What can I say?' I shrug. 'Dad's a nightmare. It's nothing new, and it's not the end of the world. You know me, I'll bounce back.'

'Of course you will. But if you ever want to talk about it . . .'

I sigh. I've done all my talking for now, but it wasn't to my girlfriend – it was to my ex. She was in the right place at the right time, and somehow the hurt and the anger I was feeling about Dad came spilling out. Now, in the cold light of morning, I wish I'd kept my mouth shut; it feels like a betrayal, somehow.

Cherry is looking at me, her dark eyes anxious. She's cute, she's kind and she cares about me far more than Honey ever did, I know. I would be crazy to screw all that up by trying to rebuild a friendship with Honey . . . not that that's what I'm doing.

Last night was a one-off.

'I don't really want to talk about it,' I say, pushing aside the guilt. 'I can't, not just now. But I know you're always there for me, Cherry . . . that means a lot.'

The bus chugs on, navigating the winding country lanes, and without warning a wave of anger and frustration washes over me; I'm trapped in this sleepy corner of Somerset for three more years at least. My days will unfold in exactly the same way as they always have done: breakfast, bus ride, school, sailing centre, maybe some time out with Cherry or a quiet hour with my guitar. It's not bad, and many people have it a whole lot worse, I know, but suddenly it's not enough.

I want to change the rules, push the boundaries, shake things up. I want to stop waiting for my life to begin and *make* things happen.

Is this how Honey feels?

'Hey,' Cherry says, nudging my arm. 'You're miles away, Shay!'

'Sorry,' I say, but a part of me wishes I was. Miles away from grumpy parents and perfect big brothers; from crazy ex-girlfriends and guilt-inducing current ones; from school and work and looming exams. With an effort, I drag my focus back to Cherry.

'I was trying to tell you about Honey's latest exploits,' she goes on. 'Boy, she's really blown it this time! Out all Sunday night and truanting school – we thought she'd run away again! Yesterday was a total nightmare – Dad and Charlotte were arguing; Skye and Summer were crying; and Coco locked herself in her room and wouldn't talk to anyone. And what does Honey do? Rage at Dad and Charlotte for calling the police and then slam out of the house and disappear again . . .'

Unease seeps through me. 'So . . . she's vanished again?' I check. 'I couldn't help noticing she's not on the bus . . .'

'Couldn't you?'

Cherry looks confused and a little hurt, and too late I realize that it's not too tactful to tell your girlfriend you've been scanning the school bus for your ex. Oops.

'Honey hasn't vanished again, Shay, so you don't

29

have to panic,' she says. 'Charlotte drove her into school for a pre-school meeting with the Head and some of her class teachers. That's why she's not on the bus. OK?'

'I just happened to notice,' I shrug. 'It's not like I was looking out for her or anything. I mean . . . why would I do that?'

Stop digging, Shay, I think. *You're in enough trouble as it is.*

'Whatever,' Cherry huffs. 'She didn't vanish, but she may as well have – she didn't get home till gone midnight, so everyone was worried sick all over again. Goodness knows where she was because Dad and Charlotte rang all her friends . . .'

I can't meet Cherry's eye, but of course she has no idea that Honey was with me. It's not something she needs to know. Ever.

The school bus shudders to a halt outside Exmoor High, and the crush of kids carries us forward and out into the bright, cool morning. Cherry's other stepsisters, the twins Skye and Summer, walk past us. Skye reaches out to swipe my beanie hat, laughing, then chucks it back at me. I struggle to dredge up a smile.

'Why would Honey even DO that?' Cherry is asking, and I seriously, seriously wish she would just drop the subject. 'Stay out so late when she was already in so much trouble? I don't get that girl,

30

not at all. It's like she WANTED them to call the police again.'

'Maybe she just wanted you all to back off,' I sigh. 'Take some time to cool down. I don't suppose she even considers what it might be like for all of you – she's hurting too much to think about anyone else.'

Cherry frowns. 'Shay, you seem to know an awful lot about what my stepsister is feeling all of a sudden!'

The air between us crackles with tension – in a year of being together, this is the closest Cherry and I have ever been to a row. She's angry, I know, and hurt too . . . Honey has made both our lives difficult over the last year. For me to start defending my ex must seem like a betrayal, but a little bit of me can't help feeling sorry for Honey. And right now I am also irritated, annoyed; with Honey, with Cherry, with myself. I wish I could rewind, start the day again.

The last thing I want is to fall out with my girlfriend.

'I don't really know how Honey feels, I'm just guessing,' I shrug, sliding an arm round Cherry's waist as we follow the crowd into school. 'It's just the way she is – most of the time she just thinks of herself, how she's feeling. Nobody else is even on her radar. That's all I'm saying . . .'

'I suppose,' Cherry says. 'Sorry, Shay, I didn't mean to be clingy. You were with Honey for months – you're bound to care about her, just a bit . . . that's only natural.'

'Hey,' I tell Cherry. 'You have nothing at all to worry about, I swear.'

'Sure,' she grins. 'I'm being silly, right? But it's just because I care.'

'I know,' I say. 'I'm sorry too . . . I'm not in the best of moods lately, as you might have noticed. Blaming my dad for that. Plus, I am shattered – I didn't get to bed till the early hours. I lay awake most of the night, but I must have dropped off in the end because I slept in and almost missed the bus. It's just not my day.'

'I bet you skipped breakfast as well,' Cherry frowns. 'You should grab something from the canteen, or you'll be tired all day. I need some stuff from my locker, but can you get me a Twix bar too? Reckon I need chocolate today!'

She hands me some silver and peels away towards the lockers while I lope along the corridor to the canteen and queue for a smoothie, a muesli bar and Cherry's Twix. The day has to get better, right? I have had enough bad luck for one lifetime, surely.

Or not.

I'm sitting on one of the tables slugging back the

smoothie when Honey Tanberry walks in, her jaw-length hair perfectly tousled, her school skirt inches shorter than every other girl's, her white shirt a shrunk-in-the-wash special. She looks a little too St Trinian's to have just come from an emergency meeting with the Head, but of course Honey makes her own rules. She's so catwalk cool and carelessly confident I guarantee nobody will have dared to challenge her.

'Sheesh,' she says, flopping down beside me. 'I hate this dump, I swear. Thanks to Mum, the teachers are going to be watching me like hawks this term. I might as well be in prison.'

She picks up the Twix I bought for Cherry, tears open the wrapper and bites a piece off.

'Hey!' I protest. 'That was for Cherry!'

'Get her another,' Honey shrugs. 'Cheers for putting up with me last night, Shay. I don't think anyone else would have had the patience to listen, and I can tell you right now that nobody else could have talked me into going home. I don't know if that's a good thing or a bad thing . . .'

'A good thing,' I say. 'Definitely.'

'Maybe. Anyhow, I just wanted to thank you for last night.'

Without warning, she flings her arms round me in a dramatic hug that has heads turning all around the canteen. I am trying to untangle myself when over her shoulder I see Cherry standing in the canteen doorway, her face frozen, her eyes wide.

I have no idea at all how long she's been there.

5

'Hang on, Cherry . . . this is NOT what it seems!'
I yelp.

Honey steps back from me, amused and
apologetic. 'Oops!' she says. 'Didn't know you were
there, stepsis!'

'Obviously,' Cherry says, her voice a whisper.

'I was just saying thank you,' Honey explains.
'Shay was a total lifesaver last night. He sat up
talking to me till all hours, then walked me home.'

My heart sinks so low it's probably in my
Converse trainers. I am in trouble – big trouble,
serious trouble.

'Cherry, I can explain,' I protest, although I'm
not sure I can.

'Don't bother,' Cherry says. 'I think I can see
what's going on.'

A small crowd of kids has gathered to gawp at
the showdown. They remember the days when I
used to date Honey and are putting two and two
together, coming up with all the wrong answers.
Just like Cherry.

'Are you cross because he didn't return your

calls?' Honey asks brightly. 'Because that was totally my fault. He wanted to, but you called right in the middle of a big heart-to-heart so I asked him not to answer . . . honestly, blame me!'

I wish the ground would open up and swallow me.

Cherry doesn't even glance at her stepsister. She looks straight at me and I can see disappointment, disgust, dismay in her eyes. I hate myself for putting those things there.

'So your phone was out of battery?' she asks quietly. 'Nice one, Shay. Next time just tell me straight that you don't want to talk to me. Except that there won't be a next time, OK?'

The kids crowded round hold their breath, and I stifle the urge to tell them all to get lost. It wouldn't help.

'Cherry, listen –'

'There's nothing you can say that I want to listen to,' Cherry says. 'Why would I believe anything you have to say? You're a liar and a cheat!'

There is no comeback to that. I am not a cheat, but a liar? Guilty as charged. I have lied to my girlfriend and been caught out; it doesn't matter that I lied for all the right reasons, to stop her from worrying, stop her from getting the wrong idea. She got the wrong idea anyhow.

'Harsh, Cherry,' Honey says, clearly amused.

'But then again . . . well, now you know how it feels.'

'Honey!' I argue. 'Cherry – it's not the same at all, if you'd just listen –'

'I've heard enough,' Cherry says, and her voice cracks a little as she speaks. 'Stay out of my way, Shay Fletcher. We're through. I never want to see you again!'

She turns on her heel and walks away, and the watching crowd whoop and cheer their support and solidarity as she goes.

'Loser,' one girl snarls at me.

'Idiot,' another spits.

The bell rings out for the first lesson, way too late to save me, and at last the crowd splinters away, heading to different corners of the building, different classes. I am left alone in the empty canteen with Honey.

'So . . . that was interesting,' she says. 'Who knew your little girlfriend could stand up for herself like that?'

'Ex-girlfriend,' I sigh. 'Thanks to you.'

'How was I to know you'd lied about your mobile?' she asks. 'And I take it you didn't tell her you were with me last night. You should have known she'd find out some time . . .'

I glare at Honey. 'Yeah, I should have known. Like I should have known you'd stir things up, make it look a million times worse than it actually was. Thanks a bunch.'

As I grab my rucksack and head to lessons, Honey shrugs and picks up the half-eaten Twix, taking another bite and wiping the chocolate from her mouth with a grin.

My life sucks, it's official. My mates Luke and Chris tell me I must be mad to go messing around with Honey again, and when I tell them I really wasn't, they smirk, disbelieving, and tell me Cherry's way too good for a Romeo like me. Skye and Summer, Honey's younger sisters, ambush me in the corridor at lunchtime, demanding to know why Cherry's so upset.

'What have you done to her?' Skye demands, furious. 'Every time I ask, she just starts crying again! There's a rumour going round that you kissed Honey in the school canteen, and if that's true I think I might have to strangle you.'

'It's not true,' I huff.

'You're not welcome in our house any more,' Summer chips in. 'You cheated on Honey last summer and ditched her for Cherry – now you've dumped Cherry! What's wrong with you, Shay? Do you enjoy hurting people?'

'I haven't – what? Of course I don't!'

But the twins turn tail and are gone.

I scrape through the day, flunking a maths test,

spilling ink all over my pencil sketch in art, breaking a guitar string in music. Yesterday's gossip about my possible contract with Wrecked Rekords has been replaced with a twisted story of how I'm way too full of myself these days and how I think Cherry's not good enough for me now.

It makes me sick.

I want to talk to Cherry, but her friends form a wall round her, warning me off. I try texting, until Cherry's friend Kira tells me to stop, that Cherry's deleted all my messages and blocked my number.

'Give up,' Kira tells me. 'Haven't you caused enough trouble?'

'It's all a mistake,' I argue. 'If I could just talk to Cherry, explain . . .'

'Take the hint,' Kira says. 'It's over.'

I make it to the end of the school day, then have to endure the bus journey home. Surprise, surprise, Cherry is not saving me a seat; she is guarded by her friends who glare at me as I mooch past, looking for somewhere to sit. Luke and Chris both live in town, so they're not around for moral support. Summer and Skye and their friends give me the cold shoulder; Alfie, who's been hanging out with us all though the holidays and has just started dating Summer, shrugs awkwardly, mouthing an apology, turning away as I pass.

'There's a spare seat here, Shay,' Honey calls

from the back, and everyone watches to see what I'll do.

I am pretty sure they'd lynch me if I took that seat, so in the end I squash in beside Anthony, a quiet loner-kid from the village, who is known as a maths and computer whizz. His hair is greasy and still cropped into a little-boy bowl-cut, his shirt is greyish and un-ironed and his school trousers flap an inch above his ankles. Anthony doesn't notice things like that, but he notices my misfortune all right.

'Hear you've blown it with Cherry,' he says brightly. 'Too bad.'

'It's a glitch,' I say. 'A misunderstanding. Trust me, it'll all be sorted by this time tomorrow.'

'How?' Anthony asks reasonably. 'As far as I can see she wants nothing to do with you.'

'I'll email,' I say confidently. 'Or send her a message on chat, or on her SpiderWeb page.'

'Don't think so,' Anthony says. 'This afternoon she was asking me how to block people on email and chat and defriend them on SpiderWeb.'

'She wouldn't do that!' I argue. 'I haven't done anything wrong!'

Anthony smiles. 'I know a lot about computers. If I wanted to, I could probably show you how to get past Cherry's security settings . . . it'd cost you, mind. But that still doesn't mean she'd read your messages. Too bad, huh?'

'Thanks for the sympathy vote,' I huff. 'If you've heard the rumours, they're all rubbish – I was just talking to Honey, that's all. It was totally innocent, like when you did that maths tutoring with her last term . . .'

He just shrugs. 'I know her better than you think,' he says. 'We're really close. Obviously, I didn't believe the rumours. I don't think anything's going on with you and Honey – but Cherry does and that's what matters. I happen to know that Honey wouldn't take you back anyway. She says you're vain and shallow –'

'*I'm* vain and shallow?' I echo. 'That's rich! This is all Honey's fault!'

'Is it?' Anthony asks. 'Are you sure?'

I scowl, staring out of the window for the rest of the journey. If I stay angry, the self-pity can't creep in, prickling my eyes with shameful tears. That can't happen, it really can't; boys don't cry.

6

I learnt not to cry early on, soon after the incident with Ben's go-cart. In my family, crying doesn't earn you sympathy or hugs, just harsh words from Dad and smirks from Ben and pitying glances from Mum. It's safer to put on a brave face, smile and hold your head high and pretend that nothing matters. You can build a wall round yourself that way, keep the hurt inside.

The trouble is, Cherry learnt the same lesson. She lost her mum when she was a little kid, and got picked on at school too; she perfected the don't-care mask, the smile that hid a whole heartful of pain. When we got together, it was pretty much the first time either of us had learnt to be open and honest with anyone else – we taught each other to trust.

I've destroyed all of that now.

Days crawl by. I fix my brave face on each morning and cycle to school – let's just say it beats the school bus. After the first day or two, I begin to enjoy the cool breeze on my face, the misty mornings, the fast pedalling along twisty moorland lanes . . . but school itself is grim.

Cherry acts like I don't exist. I knew she was hurt, I knew she was angry, but I thought she'd calm down and let me put my side of the story. I didn't think she'd shut me out, push me away, block my texts, my emails, my messages.

Why would she do that? I've messed up, I know, but surely I deserve the chance to explain?

'Maybe she was getting fed up with you anyhow,' my friend Luke says helpfully.

'Maybe she was planning to finish with you,' Chris chips in. 'Maybe all you've done was give her a good excuse.'

'Thanks, mate,' I say. 'That makes me feel a whole lot better. Not.'

'It was just an idea,' Luke shrugs.

I don't like their idea, but I start to wonder if it might be true.

Back home, I eat tea while listening to Ben's latest exploits, teach the evening kayak club at the sailing school, mop out the shower block and tidy up the reception area, hide out in the den and play guitar for hours. No matter what I do, everything seems grey and pointless without Cherry.

I sleep, and somehow I forget. I dream of moonlight and stars and sitting on the steps of the gypsy caravan with Cherry, last summer when we first met. In my dreams, the air is warm and the trees are strung with fairy lights and the two of us are talking, laughing, holding hands. We have big dreams, big hopes; and all of them are still possible.

And then I wake up, and grim reality crashes back in.

Tuesday turns into Wednesday, Wednesday into Thursday, and still Cherry won't even look at me.

What do you do when you feel so low you don't even want to lift your head up off the pillow? When your dreams of stardom bite the dust and bring you crashing down with them? When your dad treats you like dirt and your friends think you're crazy and the only girl you ever really cared about ditches you because you tried to stop your ex running away to London?

You write a song.

You stay up late night after night down by the ocean, playing sad melodies until the words you cannot say to her in the daytime fall out of your mouth and drift into the darkness, making patterns with the music, pulling the sadness from your soul and turning it into something new, something better, something beautiful.

The song is called 'Bittersweet', and it's probably the best thing I've ever done – it's a pity Cherry won't ever get to hear it.

'Bittersweet' says all the things I want to say but can't – if Cherry heard it she would understand, surely? She'd know that I'm sorry.

If I had the guts, I would pick up my guitar, walk over to Tanglewood House and play my new song in the moonlight beneath her window. The trouble is Cherry has the attic room; she might not even hear me, and knowing my luck Summer and Skye would spot me first and chuck a bucket of water over me. Or possibly boiling oil?

I sink on to a rock at the water's edge instead, pick up my guitar and start to play, losing myself in the song:

> A seagull's call cuts through the misty morning
> Sunlight hasn't touched the blankets yet . . .
> I hear your voice whisper in my waking dream,
> And tell myself you're here, and I forget –
> How yesterday your smiling eyes they left me;
> How yesterday your heart it turned away;
> Last night I dreamt of cherry-blossom trees, but now
> Comes the bittersweet reality of day . . .

As the last chorus fades away, I hear gentle clapping from behind me and jerk round to see a shadowy figure against the cliffs.. Hope floods me and I drop the guitar, scramble to my feet.

'Cherry?'

But Honey Tanberry steps out of the shadows, and my heart sinks.

'Sorry to disappoint you, Shay,' she says. 'Of

course, there was a time when you'd have been pleased to see me . . .'

'Huh,' I snap. 'What are you doing here?'

'It's a free country, isn't it? Last time I checked, this wasn't your private stretch of beach.'

I scowl. 'Haven't you caused enough trouble?'

'Me?' she echoes, wide-eyed. 'Shay, it was you who lied to Cherry!'

'But you stirred things up,' I remind her. 'And you enjoyed it.'

'Maybe I did,' she admits. 'The way I see it, Cherry had it coming – she did the same to me, didn't she?'

'It wasn't the same at all,' I say firmly. 'What happened last summer was my fault, not Cherry's, but you've never let either of us forget it. In fact, I wouldn't be surprised if this whole thing wasn't one big set-up, designed to split us up!'

'Yeah, right,' Honey huffs, her eyes flashing anger. 'Don't flatter yourself, Shay. What happened last summer is over with – I've moved on. I had way bigger things on my mind this Monday than you and your moody little girlfriend!'

I sigh, sitting down again as the truth of this sinks in.

'I guess,' I admit. 'Sorry, Honey.'

'I have to admit I've kind of enjoyed the fallout, though,' she grins. 'I didn't think you had it in you to mess up so spectacularly, Shay, but I was wrong. And Cherry is just as stupid and stubborn as you are, moping and mooning around like it's the end of the world but too proud to do anything to fix it. Too bad.'

'She's moping?' I say, suddenly hopeful. 'She misses me?'

'Like I told you, she's not very bright,' Honey shrugs. 'She misses you, but she's really hurt . . . Skye and Summer and Coco are telling her to be brave, stay strong. And none of them will talk to me! What a joke!'

'But we didn't do anything,' I argue. 'Nothing wrong, anyway!'

'Tell her that,' Honey sighs. 'I already know.'

'She won't take my calls or read my messages or texts,' I say. 'I'm doomed.'

'Maybe you're better off without her?'

Honey leans down towards me, brushing the hair from my face. Her fingers stroke my cheek, trace the shape of my lips, slide softly down my throat to rest on my collarbone. I close my eyes, my breathing suddenly ragged. I have never felt as lost or lonely as I do right now, and it would be good, so good, to hold someone close.

But the person I want to hold close is *not* Honey.

I pull back abruptly, and my ex-girlfriend laughs, tugging the beanie hat I always wear down over my face, turning the whole thing into a joke.

'Hey, you can't blame a girl for trying,' she says, flopping down on to a rock a safe distance away. 'I guess you really are missing Cherry – how else could you resist me? Better tell her, Shay. Stuff the emails and texts, be direct. Paint it in three-foot-high letters along the playing-field fence at school . . . do SOMETHING!'

'Well, I wrote her a song . . .'

'Is that what you were playing before?' she asks. 'Nice one. Mopey, but nice. Why don't you put it online and send her the link? Declare your love for all to see? She'd fall for that, I bet!'

'You think?'

'I think,' Honey says. 'Play it again and I'll film it for you and email it over. You can do whatever you like with it then.'

She perches on the rock, fiddling with her mobile, while I pick up the guitar and strum some chords. Then I start to play properly, and I forget that Honey is watching, filming. I put everything into the music . . . my heart, my soul, my feelings for Cherry.

I lose myself and find myself again.

And then the song is over, and the music lets go of me and I focus again, seeing Honey, the mobile, the empty beach, the sunset fading into darkness. Nothing is different. My life is still in ruins and my girlfriend hates me, and I am hanging out for the second time in a week with my ex, which really, seriously, cannot be a good thing.

Honey puts away her mobile, stands up.

'I'm not a total bitch, you know,' she says quietly. 'I've tried telling Cherry that nothing happened on Monday. I swore there was no funny business, but she didn't believe me. Why do people never believe me?'

I can think of a few reasons, but I say nothing. Honey is a magnet for trouble, but she has a sweet side too and right now she is trying to do something useful, something to fix up the mess the two of us have created between us.

'I'll load this on to my laptop and email it over to you,' she says. 'I hope you can patch things up. Really. And I hope your dad has a personality transplant and works out that he has two talented sons, not just one. It sucks about Wrecked Rekords.'

'It does,' I say. 'Thanks for trying to help.'

She pauses, the wind catching her hair. 'You really love her, don't you?' she says. 'Cherry. That's cute. Really. Don't mess it up.'

She turns away, and I am almost certain I can see the glint of tears in her eyes.

7

I sleep late on Friday, and as I'm scrambling into my school clothes, my mobile rings: Finch.

'Hello, mate,' I say. 'How's life in the big city?'

'Pretty dull compared to the dramas going on down your way,' he responds coolly. 'I was speaking to Skye last night. I never had you down as a love-cheat. What are you playing at, Shay?'

I sigh. How could I forget that Finch and Skye were an item? They were practically joined at the hip all summer. Looks like I just lost another friend.

'It wasn't like that,' I tell him. 'Seriously.'

'So what was it like?'

I talk to Finch and the whole story spills out: Honey threatening to run away, Cherry calling at just the wrong moment, how trying to help turned into a disaster. I tell him about the awkward moment in the school canteen when Cherry saw her stepsister's thank-you hug and got the wrong idea, how the school grapevine took it and blew it out of all proportion, turned me into a lying love-rat.

'There was really nothing in it?' Finch checks. 'What a mess. Mate, you'd better set the record straight quick because right now you are not popular with the Tanberry-Costello family.'

'Tell me about it,' I say. 'I'm not popular with anyone lately. It sucks.'

'Gotta go, mate,' Finch says. 'School's calling, and I'm helping in the studio later. They're filming the last few studio scenes for the movie. Good luck with Cherry!'

'I'll need it!'

By the time I end the call, it's too late to even think about cycling to school. Looks like I'll be braving the bus – and if I survive that, I might try yet again to screw up my courage and talk to Cherry. Finch is right – the longer I leave it, the worse it will be. Today I will swallow my pride and tell Cherry exactly what happened, even if it means grovelling a little. Or a lot.

I grab a quick smoothie in the kitchen while Mum, Dad and Ben sit down to a full-English. Dad is sorting through his post and passes a long white envelope across to Ben.

'Sheffield Hallam University,' he comments, looking at the postmark. 'What the heck do they want? You went to Birmingham!'

Ben takes the envelope and slices it open, unfolding the sheaves of paper inside. He scans the contents, smiles, then folds it up and puts it back again.

'Mistake, is it?' Dad presses. 'Just bin it, son. No worries.'

'It's not a mistake,' Ben says.

'Oh?'

'They do a great postgrad course at Sheffield,' Ben says carelessly. 'I can turn my degree into a teaching qualification.'

Dad pauses, a chunk of black pudding speared on his fork, hovering in mid-air.

'Why would you want to do that, Ben?' he asks quietly.

My brother shrugs. 'I'd like to teach,' he says. 'I've always enjoyed teaching the kids at the sailing centre, and it got me thinking about what I want to do with my life.'

Mum moves her chair back from the table and stands, scraping her half-empty plate into the bin and catching my eye with an anxious expression. I don't blame her – I'm feeling anxious too.

'You already know what you're doing with your life, Ben,' Dad is saying. 'You're going to work alongside me, at the sailing centre – and take over one day. It's understood.'

'Not by me,' Ben shrugs. 'I've never actually said that was what I wanted, Dad. I've tried to tell you about this a million times – you never listen.'

'Of course I don't,' Dad snaps. 'It's nonsense. You don't need to do a postgrad course. Why would you want to be a poxy PE teacher, running round after snotty-nosed kids? I need you here – I'm happy to give you more freedom within the business, listen to your ideas – and in a year or two I'll make you the general manager.'

'I don't think so,' Ben says. 'Helping out at the sailing centre has only ever been temporary for me. I want to teach, and this course is one of the best in the country.'

Dad looks bewildered. He is used to Ben doing exactly as he suggests – I guess we all are.

'Well,' he blusters. 'We'll talk about it. Not many young men get to walk into a managerial job in the family business. I admire your independent streak, but we're in a recession right now, son. A job means security, a future . . .'

'Dad,' Ben says patiently. 'I'm sorry. I'm going to do the postgrad course at Sheffield. It's all decided.'

'Not this year, though?' Dad argues. 'It's too late to apply now; term must be starting in a week or so.'

'I applied in January,' my brother says. 'They offered me a place and I grabbed it with both hands. I've been trying to tell you ever since . . .'

Mum steps forward with a well-timed mug of tea, aimed at calming the situation, but as she sets it down on the tabletop Dad slams his fist down, splashing tea everywhere and making his breakfast plate clatter.

'NO!' he roars at several thousand decibels. 'No, Ben, I am not going to let you do this. You'll live to regret it, and I will not let you ruin your life!'

'But, Dad,' Ben says reasonably. 'It's *my* life, surely? I'm not a kid any more, I'm twenty-one years old. I have thought this through long and hard, and it's what I want. I'm sorry but I *am* going to do it, whether you like it or not.'

'Over my dead body!' Dad roars, and his arm swipes across the tabletop, sending the breakfast plate and the mug of tea flying across the kitchen to smash into the cupboards and splatter all over the tiles.

'Go, Shay,' Mum says, stuffing my rucksack into my arms and pushing me towards the door. 'You too, Ben. Give your dad a chance to cool down . . .'

I don't need telling twice. I am out of there, grabbing my guitar and legging it out of the door. I'm running late already, and the kitchen drama hasn't helped – unless I sprint I might actually miss the school bus and earn myself a late-mark for my trouble. I am loping along the path when I hear the door slam behind me.

'Wait up, little brother,' Ben yells. 'You're cutting it a bit fine, aren't you? I'll give you a lift. C'mon . . . I could use the company!'

'OK – thanks!'

Ben's face is set, determined. He doesn't say much as we pile into his beat-up old car and drive away from the kerb, just slides the sunroof back and slots an ancient Beach Boys CD into the player and turns the volume up to max. We drive like this for ten minutes, deafened by Ben's favourite surf band churning out relentlessy happy sixties pop, before he relents and turns the volume down to bearable again.

'I am going, you know,' he says eventually. 'I'm sick of him running my life for me, controlling every little thing I do. I didn't know any better when I was your age, Shay, but I'm older now – I know what I want, and it definitely isn't this.'

'Dad'll calm down,' I say. 'I think it was just a shock for him – it was for me!'

'Yeah,' Ben sighs. 'Sorry. I should have said something to you. Mum told me to . . .'

'Mum knew?' I check, surprised.

'Yeah, of course. She's totally behind me. I've tried to talk to Dad about it loads of times, but he won't listen – he just blocks me off, changes the subject. Mum was going to break it to him gently, but . . . too late now.'

'Wow.' I blink. 'I always thought you *wanted* to run the sailing centre. I mean, I know that you wanted to be a footballer until you had that injury, but after that I was pretty sure you were set on the sailing centre. I really had no idea!'

'That was all Dad too,' Ben says, his eyes on the road. 'I liked football, but it was his passion, not mine. I was good at footy, and Dad pushed me, so I went along with it . . . until Southampton dropped me from the youth squad. That's when it all went pear-shaped.'

'Yeah, the accident,' I remember. 'That must have felt like the end of the world.'

Ben just laughs. 'Shay . . . there was no accident,' he says. 'No injury. Southampton dropped me from the squad because in the end I wasn't good enough.'

My head struggles to make sense of this.

'But you said . . .'

'Dad said,' Ben corrects me. 'He told everyone I'd had an injury because he couldn't bear to tell people the truth . . . that I just didn't make the grade. He was ashamed of me, Shay. I'd let him down.'

'Whoa,' I say. 'I never had a clue! I mean . . . you're Dad's blue-eyed boy, Ben! The favourite! He's always been so proud of you . . .'

'That's what I always thought too,' he shrugs. 'But Dad's such a control freak – he was only ever proud of me when I was doing what he said, and doing well at it. When things went wrong he lied to everyone to save face. How d'you think that felt?'

I'm guessing Ben felt the way Dad's always made me feel – a disappointment, a let-down, second best, but there is no comfort in knowing that my perfect big brother is not so perfect after all. I just feel sorry for him, and glad that he's able to get out of Kitnor and follow his own path.

I notice that Ben has driven right past the turn-off for Minehead.

'Hey – you've missed the turning!' I point out. 'Better take the next left, or I'll be late for school!'

'You're not going to school today,' Ben says. 'Lessons can wait. Dad almost ruined things for me, Shay – I'm not going to let him do the same to you. Sometimes you have to seize the moment – take the opportunities that come your way.'

'Huh?'

'Take control of your own destiny,' he says. 'Look to the future.'

'Ben, what are you talking about?'

'Wrecked Rekords,' my big brother says. 'You and I are going to London!'

8

As kidnaps go, this one is pretty cool. The morning unfolds into a road trip, with lots of brotherly bonding and advice and a long stop for Coke and chips at a greasy-spoon cafe just outside Swindon. The two of us have never talked so much before, not properly – our friendliest exchanges have always been wind-ups and jokes.

We've never been close – perhaps that was Dad's fault, or maybe it was just the age gap, but now I am getting to know my big brother and I can see he's not so very different from me. A couple of times I think of telling him about Cherry, but I don't know where to start. I want Ben's support, but not his pity.

I guess I don't need anyone else to tell me I've been an idiot. I already know.

'Dad used to play football, y'know,' he tells me. 'Small-time, Sunday league stuff. It was his dream, though. That's why he pushed me so hard – he thought he was helping me, but really it was all about him. His dream, not mine.'

'Just like the sailing centre is his thing,' I say. 'And

you're turning your back on it. That takes courage, Ben – we all know Dad has a temper on him.'

'We should have stood up to him years ago,' Ben sighs as we cruise along the M4. 'Just for the record, Shay, I'm sorry about the go-cart thing. I didn't think you'd actually go and break your arm . . .'

I laugh, and as we approach the outskirts of London I take the forms that Curtis Rawlins gave me out of my rucksack, where they've been hidden for the last few days, still slightly stained and now quite crumpled too. Can Ben really sign them for me, open up the doors to possibility again? Maybe. I hope so.

Ben makes me navigate, using a dog-eared street map and his iPhone. We get lost about a dozen times before we finally pull up outside Wrecked Rekords' Camden HQ.

It's like stepping into a dream – a dark, edgy, slightly psychotic dream. The walls are papered with silver foil and a collage of iconic album covers stretching back decades. A huge, shiny mobile made entirely from CDs spins silently in the stairwell, and framed gold discs line the hallway. Even the sofas in the waiting area look like they have been borrowed from a passing spaceship.

The girl at the reception desk has fuschia-pink hair and a pierced nose, and she seems to be wearing some kind of cool fancy-dress outfit made from a checked tablecloth and a lace curtain. She looks at me doubtfully, taking in the school uniform and beanie hat, and I flush a little pink.

I push the crumpled forms across the desk towards her, and she looks at them dubiously. 'We'd like to see Curtis Rawlins, please,' I say.

'Yeah?' the girl drawls. 'Do you have an appointment?'

'No, but . . .'

'You'll need one,' she shrugs. 'No exceptions. Why not send in a CD, some demo tracks? Then you can ring in a few weeks and if Curtis and his team think you have potential we can set you up with a November appointment. Or December, maybe. Or January.'

Or never.

Stricken, I look at Ben, who rolls his eyes dramatically. 'Don't panic, little brother,' he says under his breath. 'Leave this to me. Watch and learn . . .'

Ben leans across the desk in full-on flirt mode, his sun-gold hair flopping carelessly across his tanned face, his blue eyes intent. I am not sure that his beach-hunk looks will cut the ice with the pink-haired girl, though. She looks like she'd be more impressed with tattoos and piercings and a neon-blue mohican haircut.

'Hey,' he grins. 'The thing is . . . we've driven all

the way from Somerset. Four hours on the road, and all because Curtis wanted to see us. "Drop in any time," he said. So we did. I mean, I know that rules are rules, but we need to see the guy now, not next week or next month or next year . . .'

I hear the soft West Country burr in Ben's voice and I can tell that his charm offensive isn't working. I wonder why we didn't just wear dungarees, wellies and straw hats because to this girl we must seem like real country kids, clueless, crass.

'Aw, c'mon,' Ben pleads. 'You know what it's like. We've got the forms. You can sort this out for us – save our lives. I'd be grateful – very grateful! I'll buy you a drink after work if you like . . .'

'No, thanks,' she says.

'Look, Curtis will see us, no worries,' Ben insists. 'He's been in talks with my little brother here about signing for Wrecked. Shay's going to be the Next Big Thing!'

'They all say that,' the girl says, going back to her computer screen.

'No, seriously,' Ben presses. 'Curtis came all the way to Kitnor to see him. He's already listened to the demo tracks, and seen him play live. He wanted to sign him, but there was a bit of a mix-up. Circumstances beyond our control. But we're here to fix it now, so if you'll just let us see Curtis . . .'

'Can't,' the girl yawns. 'He's gone out. Not sure when he'll be back.'

My heart sinks. Ben's attempt to save the day has backfired, failed. We've driven all this way for nothing, but looking on the bright side, at least I got to skip a day of being glared at and frozen out at school.

We are walking out through the plate-glass doors when the miracle happens. A man in a skinny suit and a red trilby hat comes towards us, and when he sees me his face lights up.

'Shay Fletcher!' he grins. 'Great to see you! Come in, come in . . .'

He ushers us into the foyer and the fuschia-haired girl looks up from her computer screen, raising an eyebrow.

I introduce Ben and we sit on the space-age sofas while Curtis fetches us fancy cappuccinos with chocolate sprinkles and thick wedges of shortbread.

'So,' he asks me. 'What brings you all the way to London? Has your dad changed his mind?'

'Not exactly,' I admit.

'Mum supports him, though,' Ben chips in, and this is news to me. 'She's his guardian too, right? And I'll look out for him if you need me to. He'd like to go ahead and sign up, wouldn't you, Shay?'

'Well, yeah . . . I'd love to,' I say.

Curtis smiles. 'That's great, Shay,' he says. 'So . . .

you're saying that your mum would sign for you, even if it goes against your dad's wishes? Really?'

'Definitely,' Ben says. 'Maybe. Well, possibly . . .'

'No,' I admit sadly. 'I don't think she would.'

The look on Curtis Rawlins' face says it all. We are wasting his time, wasting our own. Why didn't I see that before?

'Listen,' Ben cuts in. 'I'm twenty-one and I can take charge of Shay, look after him, sign for him . . . whatever you need me to do. Dad doesn't understand and Mum won't go against him, even though she'd like to . . . but I can be the responsible adult, surely? Not everybody gets offered a chance like this. I want Shay to take it!'

I have never loved my brother more than I do right now, I swear, but Curtis sighs, and I know that Ben's suggestion isn't going to change things.

'Thing is, you're not Shay's guardian,' he says sadly. 'His parents need to be on board, and . . . well, they're not.'

'He has a talent,' Ben argues. 'You said so . . . can't you take a risk on him, bend the rules, just this once? Shay loves his music. He won't let you down!'

'I'll do whatever it takes,' I promise. 'I've got a new song – it's good, really good. Shall I play it for you?'

Curtis Rawlins shakes his head.

'I'd love to hear it, Shay, but . . . it won't make any

difference. There's nothing I'd like more than to sign you up . . . but your age is against us here. I've been talking to my colleagues. Your dad doesn't just have misgivings, he's actively hostile to the whole idea. Even if your mum was totally on board with all this I'd be very wary about taking things further right now. When we work with a minor, we need to know that the family are in, one hundred per cent. In your case, Shay, we couldn't rely on that, no matter how supportive your brother may be.'

'So . . . what are you saying?' Ben asks, frowning.

'I'm saying . . . there is nothing I would like more than to sign you to Wrecked, Shay, but right now I can't. Keep working – keep singing and writing. And come back and see me when you're eighteen.'

We shake hands with Curtis Rawlins and walk out of there with our heads held high, but inside I am shaking. I'm not sure I can take another knock without falling to pieces.

'Sorry, mate,' Ben says. 'That didn't go so well.'

'I'm sorry,' I sigh. 'I've wasted your time . . . all that effort for nothing.'

'It wasn't for nothing,' he grins. 'I got to spend some time out with my little brother, even if I had to practically kidnap you to do it. I've had fun. And it wasn't a waste – we know the situation now. You have something to work for, something to aim for.'

'I guess,' I say.

'Definitely,' Ben insists. 'We tried, didn't we? If you want something badly, you go the extra mile. You don't just sit back and accept things, you do everything you can to make it happen. Maybe it didn't work out this time, but if you keep believing, keep working, then sooner or later it will. Keep the faith. We gave it our best shot. No regrets!'

I frown. Ben is talking about the record deal, of course, but he has a point.

I think about a girl with glossy, blue-black hair, shining almond eyes fringed with long, sooty lashes, the sweetest smile. Cherry is my best friend, my crush, my confidante. Without her, everything is dull and pointless. Without her, my heart is in the gutter.

I remember Honey's advice from last night, Finch's words from this morning.

I messed up the best thing I ever had, and all over a tangle of lies and misunderstandings. I need to ditch the excuses and fix it up before it's too late. I wonder if there's time to meet Finch for a pep talk before facing Cherry, seeing as we're actually in London. I pick up my mobile to message him and find it's dead, out of charge. Looks like I'm on my own with this.

What was it Ben said? If you want something badly, you go the extra mile.

9

Ben and I mooch around Camden for a while, checking out the quirky stalls and eating pitta bread and falafel down by the canal in the sunshine. I remember Honey's pipe dream of running away and starting a fashion stall here, and sigh. Ben buys a couple of T-shirts and I buy a second-hand silver chain with a cherry-motif pendant, hoping I get the chance to give it to Cherry. We both pick out mirrored sunglasses and drive out of Camden at sunset with the sunroof down and Ben's Beach Boys CD blaring.

We don't get home till midnight.

Dad appears in the doorway the minute Ben's car pulls up, the anger rolling off him in waves. I can feel my shoulders slump.

Today is the day I learnt how cool my brother really is, and the day I found out for sure that I will not be a fifteen-year-old teen idol signed up to Wrecked Rekords. It's the day I discovered that the best things in life are worth fighting for, that if you don't like something you change it.

It was a life-changing day, but now, back home, it

feels like nothing has altered at all. Dad unleashes his temper, ranting about how Ben and I have let him down, left him short-staffed, had everyone worried sick.

Yeah, right.

Following Ben down the garden path, I stop abruptly and turn, dropping my schoolbag into the flower bed and shrugging my guitar over one shoulder. I walk away, Dad yelling my name into the darkness.

For once, I just don't care.

I walk through the silent village, street-lamp spooky, and out along the dark lane that leads to Tanglewood. The sky is scattered with stars and my eyes adjust quickly to the dark, but I am scared. What if it all goes wrong, if Cherry won't see me, if Paddy and Charlotte set the dog on me or call the police?

Don't just sit back and accept things, I remember. *Go the extra mile.*

What's the worst that could happen?

I push the gate open and crunch across the gravel, beneath trees hung with solar-powered fairy lights, a leftover from the summer. The house is in darkness, silent, sleeping. I hear Fred the dog barking from inside the house and Humbug the sheep bleating from his stable, but I walk on until I am positioned beneath Cherry's attic window.

Picking up a handful of gravel, I throw one small pebble upwards in a swift arc and hear the satisfying clink of stone on glass.

A light goes on, but it's the wrong light. The room Skye and Summer share. Great.

The twins appear at the window, then the sash slides up and Skye leans out.

'Shay?' she whispers. 'What the . . . ?'

'Shhh,' I say. 'Please? I know what you think of me, Skye, but give me a chance – I just need Cherry to hear me out.'

'Finch rang me this afternoon,' she says softly. 'He explained. To be fair, Honey'd been saying the same thing too, but we didn't listen . . .'

'You're speaking to me?' I ask, wide-eyed. 'You believe me?'

Summer leans out of the window alongside her twin.

'Of course we do,' she says. 'We've been texting you all day . . . Cherry has too!'

'She has?' I grin. 'My mobile's dead. Sorry!'

'No, we're sorry,' Summer says. 'We should have given you a chance. It's just – Cherry's cool. She's our stepsister, and she's had a rough time, and nobody – NOBODY – is allowed to hurt her.'

'I wouldn't,' I argue. 'I won't!'

'Better tell her that,' Skye laughs.

I take another piece of gravel and aim higher,

but this time the pebble hits the roof and skids down the slates again with a clatter. Abruptly, the turret room lights up and Honey's window swings open.

'About time,' she calls down. 'Have I missed the big apology?'

'No,' I huff. 'Give me a chance. I wasn't counting on having an audience . . .'

'Too bad,' Honey drawls. 'You've woken us up, you'd better entertain us now.'

Another light snaps on, over to the right, and Coco's window creaks open. 'Is that you, Shay?' she wants to know.

'Who else would it be?' Skye yells across. 'We don't usually have random teenage boys wandering about the garden in the middle of the night, do we?'

'You never know, with you lot!' Coco smirks. 'This is SO slushy! Are you serenading her, Shay? Romeo, Romeo, wherefore art thou, Romeo?'

'Cut it out,' I say. 'It's not funny!'

'It is from where I'm standing,' Honey says, and Coco pushes her window open wider, settling herself on the window sill with her violin. A whining dirge begins to swirl out into the darkness, and in the kitchen Fred the dog begins to whine along in tune. On the plus side, if the pebble-throwing doesn't wake Cherry, the violin solo definitely will. Ouch.

The downstairs lights flare into life, the kitchen door opens and Paddy and Charlotte appear on the doorstep in PJs and dressing gowns.

'What the heck is going on?' Paddy demands. 'Is this some kind of midnight garden party, or are you just casing the joint for a possible burglary? Shay?'

'I can explain,' I say, alarmed. 'If I could just talk to Cherry . . .'

'Finally,' Charlotte says. 'Can you two just make up, please? I can't take any more of the tears and moping.'

'Somebody wake Cherry, for goodness' sake,' Honey grumbles. 'We'll be here all night.'

Finally the light goes on in Cherry's attic room, and the Velux window lifts and opens and a sad, pale face framed with dark, rumpled hair appears above me.

'Say something then,' Coco says, setting down her violin at last. 'She's waiting!'

They're all waiting. I know I need to apologize, but not to the whole family, surely?

I clear my throat. 'Cherry?' I call up to her. 'I think we need to talk. I . . . I've messed up and there's a lot I need to say to you, but . . . it's hard to find the right words. So . . . well, I wrote a song. For you.'

I take a deep breath.

'Go for it, Shay,' Honey says. 'What are you waiting for?'

So I play. I try to forget that Cherry's dad and stepmum are right in front of me, that Fred the dog is sniffing around my feet, that her stepsisters are watching, that my ex-girlfriend is listening. I blank it all out and keep my eyes on Cherry, putting my heart and soul into the song.

When I finish, there is a silence and Cherry puts a hand to her mouth and ducks away from the window, out of sight.

Then Skye and Summer begin to clap, and Coco whoops and whistles, and even Honey, Paddy and Charlotte join in. Fred licks my hand and wallops the blue guitar with his tail.

At last Cherry appears in the kitchen doorway and her stepsisters vanish, one by one, their lights extinguished like candles on a birthday cake.

'Don't be too late,' Paddy says, and he and Charlotte retreat too, leaving Cherry and me alone. In the shadows outside the kitchen door we are awkward, unable to look at each other.

'I'm sorry,' I blurt.

'No, I'm sorry –'

'It was all a mistake – I know I shouldn't have blanked your call – but there was honestly *nothing* going on . . .'

'I know,' she says. 'Honey swore the same thing.

And Skye said you told Finch the whole story . . .'

'I should have told *you*, though,' I sigh. 'I'm an idiot.'

'I'm an idiot too, for not trusting you . . . it's just that it looked bad, and I was so upset and didn't want to listen . . . I felt so stupid!'

'No, I'm the stupid one . . .'

We move away from the house, in case well-meaning stepsisters are eavesdropping in darkened rooms. We walk down beneath the trees strewn with fairy lights and sit on the steps of the gypsy caravan, the way we used to last summer when we first met, before we were actually going out together.

'You wrote a song for me,' Cherry says. 'It's beautiful.'

'You're beautiful,' I say. 'The song doesn't even start to say what I'd like to say, but it was terrible without you . . . I'm going to make sure I don't lose you again, OK? No matter what.'

'I'm not beautiful, though,' Cherry protests. 'I'm just ordinary, really, and Honey – well, she really is gorgeous. That's why I thought . . . maybe you'd had enough of me, maybe you wanted to be with her again . . .'

'You're a million miles from ordinary, Cherry,' I sigh. 'You're the most beautiful girl in the world to me, inside and out. I never felt that way about

Honey, not ever. I cared about her, sure – I still do because she's so mixed up, so unhappy. She was in pieces about the threat of being taken into care, threatening to run away again – I don't know why she came to me, but she did, and I had to at least try to help. I had no idea it would all turn into such a mess, or I wouldn't have bothered . . .'

'You would, though,' Cherry says. 'Because you're kind and caring and thoughtful. That's why I love you.'

When I hear those words I don't care any more about the ruined record deal or wasted trip to London or the fact that Dad will probably ground me for the rest of my life when I finally go back home. I don't even care that I've just had the worst few days of my whole entire life because I know that everything is going to be OK again. Better than OK.

Cherry leans up and kisses me, and I want the kiss to go on forever, warm lips, the taste of mint toothpaste, happiness. We pull apart and sit for a long time on the caravan steps beneath the cherry trees, arms wrapped round each other.

'We'll be OK, won't we?' I ask at last.

'We'll be fine,' Cherry says. 'Promise. But . . . will you play that song again? "Bittersweet"? Please?'

So I do.

10

I get home at daybreak, and Dad yells and roars and tells me I am grounded until Christmas, except for school and my job at the sailing centre. I shrug. Nothing he says or does can touch me now.

When I don't react, he takes away my mobile phone and bans me from the internet, even says he'll put my blue guitar on the bonfire.

'No,' Mum argues. 'Enough! I won't stand for it, Jim. That's plain cruel. You've pushed one son away – don't do the same to Shay!'

I don't remember Mum ever standing up to Dad before, certainly not to defend me. Dad looks just as shocked.

'I just want what's best for him!' he protests. 'He'll thank me, one day!'

'Like Ben is thanking you?' Mum asks. 'You have two wonderful, talented sons – but you can't see that because all their lives you've been trying to bully and control them, push square pegs into round holes. You've spent years trying to turn Ben into a carbon copy of you, but you'll never do it – he's different, can't you see that?

'You've ignored Shay because you don't understand him, which is just as bad. Perhaps he is too young for the music business right now, but you can't crush his dreams just because they're different from yours. He's going to shine, with or without your help!'

Dad's face struggles between anger and irritation, finally settling on disgust.

'I didn't mean it, about the guitar,' he grates out. 'I'm not a tyrant, you know. I just want what's best for them!'

'Then let them make mistakes, and learn from them,' Mum says. 'The way we did. You have to stop this, Jim. Let them have the freedom to be whoever they want to be, and be proud of them for that.'

Dad rolls his eyes and stomps away. In the end, he leaves me with my guitar but sticks with the mobile/internet ban. Mum stops talking to him, except in front of the sailing-centre clients. She stops bringing him cups of tea, gives up ironing his shirts, abandons the morning fry-ups.

It goes on for a week.

In fifteen years, I have never known Mum to protest at all, but now she is making her feelings clear, and Dad is not impressed. You could cut the atmosphere at home with a knife.

It's actually a relief to be at school. I hang out in the music room at lunchtimes with Cherry, but the other kids are talking to me again – all is forgiven. They ask if I've signed the contract with Wrecked Rekords yet; when I tell them there is no record contract, they look disbelieving, like I am trying to hide my imminent fame and fortune from them. It's like they are expecting me to pop up on *X Factor* any day now.

'Love the new song,' one kid says. I can't help noticing he's wearing a beanie hat just like mine.

'Brilliant stuff,' a girl chips in.

'What are you talking about?' I frown. 'How...?'

'"Bittersweet",' the beanie-hat kid says. 'Awesome.'

'Have you been telling people about the song?' I ask my mate Chris at lunchtime. 'Kids keep asking me about it. I mean, how do they even know?'

'Hard to miss, these days,' he says, grinning. 'You have a lot of support, Shay.'

'Everyone knows who you are now,' Luke cuts in. 'You've gone way up in the popularity stakes, I kid you not. All the Year Ten girls are crushing on you, and I counted seven kids wearing beanie hats in the canteen yesterday lunchtime. Jammy swine – how did you manage to get so lucky?'

'All hope of a recording contract shot down in flames,' I remind him. 'Grounded till Christmas? Mobile confiscated? Banned from the internet? How is that lucky, exactly?'

'You're obviously getting round the internet ban somehow, though,' Chris says. 'Your music page on SpiderWeb is updated every day . . .'

I frown. 'Hang on . . . I don't have a page on SpiderWeb!'

'You definitely do,' Luke insists. 'That song you wrote for Cherry is on there. "Bittersweet". Nice one!'

'The page has loads of "likes",' Luke tells me. 'People commenting and stuff. It's good!'

'But . . . I don't get it! I haven't made a music page!' I argue.

Luke takes out his iPhone and searches the net, and sure enough up comes a page called 'Shay Fletcher Music'. There's a photo of me, a moody black-and-white snapshot of me playing guitar by a beach bonfire. I've never seen the picture before, but I know it's from the summer, from one of the beach parties we had. Who took it?

Just as Chris and Luke said, a video of 'Bittersweet' is on there; the shadowy, grainy film Honey took of me down by the shore. Someone has ramped up the contrast and chopped the editing around a bit, and the whole thing looks pretty awesome for something recorded so quickly. There's a sort of home-made cool to it, and the sound is actually pretty good.

The video has hundreds of comments, and the page itself has almost 1,200 'likes'.

'Who put all this together?' I puzzle. 'And how has it got all these followers so quickly? I don't get it! I only wrote the song last week!'

We scroll through the comments, all good; some of the names I recognize – Cherry, Skye, Summer, Alfie, Finch . . . plus lots of kids from school and even our maths teacher, Mr Farrell. Others are names I don't know at all.

'That's how the internet works,' Chris shrugs. 'Things snowball. Some musicians don't actually need a record deal to make the big time these days, you must know that!'

My head spins with questions . . . Honey took the video of me singing 'Bittersweet', but would she go to all the trouble of making a page to promote it? I'm not convinced. Cherry, maybe? Honey must have given her the video.

'I love that fanpage on SpiderWeb,' I tell her on the school bus home. 'I can't believe you'd do that for me!'

'I didn't.' She smiles mysteriously, sliding the little cherry pendant I bought her up and down on its silver chain. 'Someone's on your side, though. Someone who knows a lot about you. It's so cool . . . and you're getting loads of "likes"! Everyone I know is sharing the link!'

'OK . . . that's great! But . . . it's definitely not you?' I check.

'Not me. I thought it was Ben, maybe?'

'I don't think so . . . not really his style.'

Cherry shrugs. 'I don't suppose it matters who it is . . . It's taking off, and that's what counts! You never know just who might hear that song . . . if you know what I mean!'

'Um . . . I don't, actually,' I say.

'Never mind,' she says cryptically. 'You'll find out soon enough, if things work out the way we think . . .'

'Huh? Cherry, you can't just say stuff like that and leave me hanging!'

'Don't listen to her,' Skye says, leaning across the aisle. 'She's talking rubbish. Just trying to confuse you. It might all come to nothing . . .'

'What might?' I growl. 'You're not making any sense!'

'Be patient!' Summer chimes in. 'If it happens, it happens. If it doesn't . . . well, no harm done. Don't worry, Shay!'

The three of them giggle and whisper and nudge each other, refusing to say anything more.

The next day, my brother Ben moves out. He packs his little car up with a suitcase and a couple of boxes, scrawls his address on a scrap of paper and hands me fifty quid.

'If you can't stick it, jump on a train to Sheffield

and come find me,' he says. 'I mean it, mate. I'm there for you, whenever, whatever.'

'Thanks, Ben.'

'If Dad's still being an idiot, or school sucks, or even if you just fancy another road trip . . .'

I laugh. 'I know. I'll miss you,' I grin, and my big brother hauls me in for a big bear hug. I wonder why it has taken me fifteen years to see just how amazing he really is?

'Seriously,' he says. 'Don't let the old man push you around the way he did with me. You always were better at standing up to him than I was. Be strong. Be your own person.'

'I will, promise.'

Mum hugs Ben next, wiping away tears. 'He's a silly, stubborn man,' she tells Ben. 'But he loves you very much. He'll come round.'

'I know,' Ben says. He gets into the car and starts the engine, idling a little as he looks up beyond us to the cottage. I can't imagine what he must be feeling – a jumble of emotions, good and bad, for the man who tried to live his own dreams through him.

At the very last minute Dad comes down the path, his face like stone. Ben winds down the car window. 'I hope you don't live to regret this, son,' he mutters. 'I think you're making a big mistake.'

Ben just smiles. 'It'll all work out. I wish it could be different, Dad, but . . . no regrets.'

As the car pulls away, Dad shades his eyes with one hand, watching until the battered VW vanishes over the hill.

'Still proud of you, Ben,' he says gruffly. 'Always.'

He slings an arm round my shoulders. 'Come on, son. We've got classes to take at the sailing centre, trippers to take out. Let's get going.'

We work hard, and as the day wears on I notice a thaw between Mum and Dad. Cups of tea appear between classes, smiles are exchanged, words spoken. It's like the coming of the spring after an arctic winter, slow but sure.

We're just clearing up after the last of the punters has gone when two cars pull into the car park in a squeal of gravel. One of them is Paddy's little red minivan, the other a sleek, silver Citroën like the one Finch's mum drives. Paddy, Charlotte, Cherry, Skye, Summer and Coco pile out of the red van, and Finch and his mum Nikki spring out of the Citroën.

I stop dead just outside the shower block, mop and bucket in hand.

'What . . . is something up? What's wrong?'

'Nothing's *wrong*,' Cherry tells me. 'Just the opposite. We have good news!'

'We've been talking to your parents,' Nikki explains. 'Over the last few days. And we think we have come to an agreement, but of course you'd have to be up for it too . . .'

'Up for what?' I ask.

Mum and Dad appear in the reception doorway.

'We got the final go-ahead,' Nikki tells them. 'I thought we should come and tell you in person. Tell Shay.'

'Tell me what?'

'I saw your new song on the internet,' Finch takes up the story. '"Bittersweet". It's amazing . . . totally the best thing you've done. Just full of feeling. And the more I played it the more I realized it would be absolutely perfect . . .'

'Perfect for what?' I frown.

'The film,' Nikki says. 'We've finished shooting now, so it's just a matter of editing and putting it all together. We had a few pieces of music in mind for the title sequence, but nothing as powerful as your piece, Shay. We'd like to use it – the message echoes the storyline in our film perfectly, and we'd pay you, of course!'

I blink, waiting for the news to sink in, start making sense. It doesn't.

I look at Cherry, Skye, Summer; they knew, of course. I remember the whispered hints, the giggles, the smiles. But Mum and Dad? Could they have known too? I notice the glint of pride in Dad's eye, the relief in Mum's smile. This is something they've been arguing about, perhaps for days. Somehow, miraculously, they've come to an agreement.

'I can see it could be a good opportunity, son,' Dad says. 'We'll put the money away for you, for when you're old enough to use it for something sensible.'

'No way,' I say. 'You're OK with it? Really?'

'Really,' Mum grins. 'If it's what you want, Shay?'

'It's what I want,' I blurt. 'Definitely, totally. I mean . . . whoa!'

'This won't be the same as signing to a big record label,' Nikki points out. 'It's a much gentler way to make your mark. You'll get a lot of exposure, but it'll be all about the music itself . . . not about turning you into some kind of teen pop idol. Your parents are much more comfortable with that idea.'

Dad raises an eyebrow, as if he's not too sure at all, but is doing his best to live with it. 'Might all come to nothing,' he says gruffly. 'But if you end up being famous, remember your old dad, won't you?'

He smiles cautiously, and fifteen years of mis-understandings begin to fall away. It doesn't matter, not now. With families, it is never too late to start over.

Much later, I am walking over to the storeroom den at sunset, the blue guitar slung over one shoulder, when I see a lone figure down on the shore. Honey is looking out at the horizon, her blonde choppy bob ruffling in the breeze, arms wrapped around herself in the chill evening.

'Hey,' I call, and Honey turns, snapping out of her dream. 'I just wanted to thank you.'

'Thank me? For what?'

'Well . . . I think you made that music page on SpiderWeb,' I say quietly. 'And the page went a bit crazy . . .'

'Viral,' Honey supplies. 'Not me, though. I don't have time for good deeds, or the internet – I spend all my spare time studying these days.'

'Yeah, right!' I grin. 'Anyway, lots of people saw it, including Finch and his mum . . . they got the TV people to listen, and now it turns out that "Bittersweet" is going to be the opening soundtrack on that movie they were making. It fits in with the theme, apparently. You probably know all this . . . half your family came over to the sailing centre earlier, with Finch and Nikki, to tell me the news. The best bit is, Dad finally stopped being pig-headed and he's going to let me do it . . .'

'I knew something was going on,' Honey says. 'Your luck turned then?'

'I guess. And I have you to thank because you took the video, and I'm pretty sure you posted it online. Everyone's been talking about it but nobody seems to know who's behind it . . . Cherry and the others thought it was Ben, but he'd have

84

said. Besides, he doesn't even have SpiderWeb.'

'What does it matter who made the page?' she shrugs. 'Just leave it. One of life's great mysteries.'

'I've solved it,' I smile. 'I loved what you did with the video – very arty.'

'Thanks,' she says. 'Best if they think Ben made it, though. We don't want you getting into trouble again, do we?'

'That won't happen. Cherry and me, we're fine now – unbreakable.'

'Right,' Honey says. 'Well. That's . . . good.'

I catch the bright glint of tears in her eyes and look away, embarrassed. When I glance up again there's no trace of sadness, just perfectly painted eyeliner, a glossy smile, the cool, hard look I know so well.

'Run along, Shay,' she tells me. 'You know what happens when you're seen hanging out with me. I'm bad news. Trouble. Selfish to the bone.'

'I don't believe that.'

'I know you don't,' Honey says, and the ghost of a smile flickers across her face. 'You never did, and I sometimes think you were the only one. But trust me, Shay . . . some things are better left unsaid.'

She turns and walks away along the sand, back towards Tanglewood, and she doesn't look back.

Now you've enjoyed Summer, it's time to
love her little sister Coco's story.

Read on for a sneak preview of
the next gorgeous book in

the chocolate box girls

COCO
Caramel

I set up a table in the foyer of Exmoor Park Middle School, cover it with a red-and-white checked cloth and drape my hand-painted banner, SAVE THE GIANT PANDA, across the front of it. Then I set out the plates and arrange my home-baked cupcakes, which I have iced with little black-and-white panda faces. Who could resist?

'They look better than the whale ones you made last time,' my friend Sarah comments. 'These ones are actually quite cute. What are we charging? Ten pence? Twenty pence?'

'Thirty pence, or two for fifty pence,' I decide. 'It's for charity, isn't it?'

It is the first day back after the October holiday and Sarah and I have been allowed out of history ten minutes early to

❀❀❀❀❀❀❀❀❀❀❀❀❀❀❀❀❀❀❀❀❀❀

set up our stall, so that we can make the most of the break-time rush once the bell goes.

Sarah unpacks a Tupperware box of chocolate fridge cake and I set out a slightly dented Victoria sponge, a tin of chocolate crispy cakes and a tub of rock buns that are a little too rock-like for comfort. My friends always rally round at times like this and manage to contribute something. I arrange my handmade leaflets, explaining why the giant panda is endangered and needs our help. I have learnt the hard way that my fellow pupils are rarely impressed by my efforts to raise funds with sponsored walks or silences. They are much more likely to part with their cash if cake is involved.

'OK,' Sarah says. 'Thirty seconds and counting. Watch out for those Year Six boys – I'm sure they nicked my flapjacks last time!'

'Nobody will dare swipe so much as a crumb while I'm watching,' I promise. I pull on my fake fur panda hat with the sticky-up ears and square my shoulders, ready to do battle.

'Here we go,' I say to Sarah. 'For the pandas!'

The bell goes and the foyer floods with kids. They can scent cake, and they swarm around the stall, grabbing panda cupcakes and wedges of Victoria sponge, shoving warm, sticky coins into the collection tin.

❀❀❀❀❀❀❀❀❀❀❀❀❀❀❀❀❀❀❀❀❀❀❀

One cute little Year Five girl buys up the whole tin of chocolate crispy cakes for £5, because it's her mum's birthday. Then I spot a weaselly Year Six boy trying to pocket a couple of chunks of chocolate fridge cake and grab his wrist firmly. 'Fifty pence, please,' I say sweetly. 'All proceeds go to help the giant panda!'

'Help it do what?' he asks, reluctantly handing over his cash.

'Survive,' I explain patiently. 'They are almost extinct, because bamboo forests are being cut down and pandas eat mainly bamboo shoots.'

'Why don't they eat something different then?' the kid asks. 'Fish 'n' chips. Big Macs. Chocolate fridge cake.'

I roll my eyes. 'They can't,' I explain. 'They are PANDAS, not people. They are supposed to eat bamboo shoots, and people are destroying their habitat. It's up to us to save them!'

The boy's face hardens. 'If that's true, you really shouldn't wear a panda hat,' he says. 'That's just sick.' He walks away, scoffing fridge cake.

Boys really are infuriating and dim, especially Year Six boys.

And Year Eight boys are not much better. Lawrie Marshall has edged his way to the front of the crowd and is reading my panda leaflet with a sneery, disgusted look on his face.

✿✿✿✿✿✿✿✿✿✿✿✿✿✿✿✿✿✿✿✿✿✿✿

Lawrie is the scratchiest, surliest boy I've ever met. He's a loner, radiating waves of simmering anger that keep both kids and teachers at arm's length. If he were a chocolate truffle, he'd be one of Paddy's disastrous experiments – dark chocolate filled with gherkins and liquorice, or something equally horrific.

He must have a sweet tooth, though, because he always turns up at my cake sales.

'How come you think you can change the world with cake?' he snarls, bundling four cupcakes into a paper bag and handing over a pound coin.

'I just do,' I say. 'I care about the pandas, and anything I can do to raise awareness and raise money has got to help.'

'Huh,' Lawrie says. 'What's the black-and-white icing supposed to be, anyway? Badgers?'

'Panda faces,' I say through gritted teeth. 'Obviously.'

'Right,' he grunts. 'Don't give up the day job, OK?'

I roll my eyes.

'Like the hat,' Lawrie sneers, stalking away. I resist the temptation to throw a rock bun at the back of his head – but only just.

'Ignore him,' Sarah says. 'He has a chip on his shoulder.'

✿✿✿✿✿✿✿✿✿✿✿✿✿✿✿✿✿✿✿✿✿✿

'A what?'

She shrugs. 'You know – it's just one of those things that people say. He's angry at the world. Snippy with everyone. Don't take it personally.'

The teachers drift over, buying the last few cakes for the staffroom, and I hand out the remaining leaflets to anyone who will take one.

'There has to be twenty quid in there, at least,' Sarah says, grinning at the collection tin, and suddenly I feel doubtful, disappointed. Twenty quid isn't a whole lot really, especially considering all the flour and eggs and sugar and food colouring I've forked out to make my cupcakes. It's not enough to save the giant panda, I am pretty sure. Looking around the table, I notice half a dozen discarded panda leaflets lying on the ground, and my spirits dip still further.

Saving the world with cake may actually be harder than I thought.

I glare at Lawrie Marshall as he stomps away along the corridor. I don't think he has a chip on his shoulder so much as a whole plateful of the things, drenched in vinegar.

❀❀❀❀❀❀❀❀❀❀❀❀❀❀❀❀❀❀❀❀❀❀❀❀

Are you a *Cathy Cassidy* superfan?

Can't wait to discover all the news about Cathy and her amazing books?

Then the brand new

is for you!

Tune in and you can:

- ▶ Watch video blogs from **CHERRY**, **SKYE**, **SUMMER**, **COCO**, **HONEY** and **SHAY**

- ▶ See a **NEW** video every time you visit

- ▶ Enter fun surveys to win **FAB** prizes

- ▶ See Cathy Cassidy read from her books and answer **YOUR** questions

- ▶ Watch book trailers, music videos and much, much more!

Visit **www.youtube.com/CathyCassidyTV** today!

The scrumptious series by

Cathy Cassidy

The Chocolate Box GIRLS

Cherry:
Dark almond eyes, skin the colour of milky coffee, wild imagination, fiesty, fun ...

Skye:
Wavy blonde hair, blue eyes, smiley, individual, kind ...

Summer:
Slim, graceful, pretty, loves to dance, determined, a girl with big dreams ...

Coco:
Blue eyes, fair hair, freckles, a tomboy who loves animals and wants to change the world ...

Honey:
Willowy, blonde, beautiful, arty and out of control, a rebel ...

Each sister has a different story to tell, which will be your favourite?

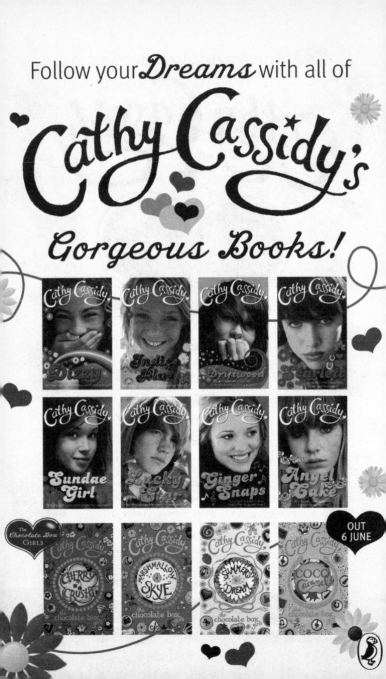

When you grow up you want to be . . .

a) an interior designer
b) a vet
c) a writer
d) a prima ballerina
e) famous

People always compliment your . . .

a) individuality. If anyone can pull it off you can!
b) caring nature – every creature deserves a bit of love
c) wild imagination . . . although it can get you into trouble sometimes
d) determination. Practice makes perfect
e) strong personality. You never let anyone stand in your way

Mostly As . . . *Skye*
Cool and eclectic, friends love your relaxed boho style and passion
for all things quirky.

Mostly Bs . . . *Coco*
A real mother earth, but with your feet firmly on the ground, you're
happiest in the great outdoors – accompanied by a whole menagerie
of animal companions.

Mostly Cs . . . *Cherry*
'Daydreamer' is your middle name . . . Forever thinking up crazy stories and
buzzing with new ideas, you always have an exciting tale to tell – you're
allowed a bit of artistic licence, right?

Mostly Ds . . . *Summer*
Passionate and fun, you're determined to make your dreams come
true . . . and your family and friends are behind you every step of the way.

Mostly Es . . . *Honey*
Popular, intimidating, lonely . . . everyone has a different idea about the
'real you'. Try opening up a bit more and you'll realize that friends are there
to help you along the way.

Cathy Cassidy's

Rocking Rocky Road Recipe – with Marshmallows!

You will need:

2 medium-sized bars of milk chocolate
A couple of handfuls of mini marshmallows
6 digestive biscuits (broken into largish chunks)
A handful of raisins (optional)

💜 Melt the chocolate in a bowl over a pan of simmering water

💜 Once the chocolate has melted, leave it to cool slightly then add the rest of the ingredients and mix well (but make sure that you don't break up the biscuits too much)

💜 Pour the mix into a baking tray, which has been lined with baking parchment, level out and put in the fridge for a few hours

💜 Once the mix has set, tip it out of the tin and cut into squares, make yourself a cup of hot chocolate and enjoy!

Summer Fruit Skewers

For a refreshing healthy snack on those hot summer days, try making your own garden of fruit skewers.

You will need:

Your fave fruits (the best ones include kiwis, strawberries, grapes, oranges, and watermelon and pineapple slices)

10 or more wooden skewers

Heart, flower or butterfly cookie cutters

A shoe box (this will be your garden display)

What to do:

Using a chopping board carefully cut your chosen fruit into round shapes.

One at a time, lay your slices of fruit on the board and cut into flower, butterfly and heart shapes using the cookie cutters.

Carefully insert the skewers into the fruit to create a beautiful flower display.

Making a Flower:

Cut a slice of pineapple into a flower shape and add to the skewer so it's horizontal. Then add a small strawberry to the very top to make the centre of the flower. Add a couple of grapes to the 'stem' of the flower to look like leaves. Try other methods and designs too!

Top Tip!
For an extra-refreshing taste, serve with a yoghurt or cream-cheese dip!

Assemble Your Flower Garden:

Decorate your shoe box to make it look like a garden, using green paint, tissue paper, flower stickers, etc.

Cut small holes into the top of the shoe box.

Insert your flower skewers into the holes to create a flower border!

If you enjoyed
Bittersweet,
here are Cathy Cassidy's *Top 10*
books that you might like too!

Stargirl by Jerry Spinelli
You Don't Know Me by David Klass
How I Live Now by Meg Rosoff
Once by Morris Gleitzman
The Weight of Water by Sarah Crossan
Love, Aubrey by Suzanne La Fleur
Born to Run by Michael Morpurgo
Solace of the Road by Siobhan Dowd
Broken Soup by Jenny Valentine
Along for the Ride by Sarah Dessen

Plus!

COCO
Caramel
by
Cathy Cassidy

OUT
JUNE
2013

BOOKs rock!

Want to read more?

VISIT your local bookshop

- Get great recommendations for books you'll love
- Meet your favourite authors & illustrators at brilliant events
- Discover books you never knew existed!

www.booksellers.org.uk/bookshopsearch

JOIN your local library

You can browse and borrow from a huge selection of books and get recommendations of what to read next from expert librarians – all for FREE!

You can also discover libraries' wonderful children's and family reading activities – such as reading groups (*see* www.chatterbooks.org.uk), author events and challenges (*see* www.summerreadingchallenge.org.uk).

Get Online

Explore www.worldbookday.com to discover a world of bonkersly brilliant beautiful books!

- Downloads and activities for your favourite books and authors
- Cool games, trailers and videos
- Fantastic competitions
- Author events in your area
- Sign up for the **FREE** monthly e-newsletter

And much, much more...

Sponsored by
National Book Tokens

WORLD
BOOK
DAY

7 MARCH 2013

Win!

£100 of BOOKS
each for *you* and
your school!

All you have to do is answer one VERY important question.

Imagine you're travelling to a *far away planet*, or a *desert island*, or even a *desert* . . . and, wherever you're going, there are **NO BOOKS**. Luckily, you're allowed to take just **ONE** book with you on your journey. What would it be?

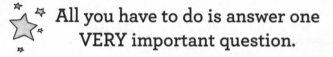

Win! For your chance to **WIN**, just tell us the name of your chosen book!

To enter go to **www.worldbookday.com**

What *Cathy Cassidy's* fans think ...

'I LOVE your books ... I can't put them down' *Leyla*

'I can't wait until *Coco Caramel*!
You're my favourite author EVER!!' *Ellen*

'I can't wait till your other books come out
The Chocolate Box Girls are the best!' *Ruby*

'Me and my best friend have read all of your books!' *Isabelle*

'I'm obsessed with reading your books – they are
just THE BEST! You rock Cathy!' *Momin*

More praise for Cathy!

'I was addicted to *Marshmallow Skye* ... beautiful,
perfect and super moreish' **thebookaddictedgirl.blogspot.com**

'Writing as engaging as this is not easy to pull off' *Mail on Sunday*

'A great choice for older Jaqueline Wilson fans' *Irish Independent*

'Wittily written ... from the heart' *Radio Times*

Write your own review at www.cathycassidy.com

OUT
6 JUNE

Catch all the latest
news and gossip from

Cathy Cassidy

at

www.cathycassidy.com

✦ Sneaky peeks at new titles

✦ Details of signings and events near you

✦ Audio extracts and interviews with Cathy

✦ Post your messages and pictures

Which Chocolate Box Girl Are You?

Your perfect day would be spent . . .

a) visiting a busy vintage market
b) with your favourite canine companion on a long walk in the countryside
c) curled up on the sofa watching black-and-white movies with your boyfriend
d) window-shopping with your BFF
e) sipping frappuccinos in a hip city cafe

Your ideal boy is . . .

a) arty and sensitive
b) boy? No thanks!
c) a good listener . . . and a little bit quirky
d) polite and clever
e) good looking and popular – what other kind of boy is there?

Who's the first person you would tell about your new crush?

a) your sister – she knows everything about you
b) your pet cat . . . animals are great listeners
c) your BFF
d) your mum – she always has the best advice
e) no one. It's best not to trust anyone with a secret

Your favourite subject is . . .

a) history
b) science
c) creative writing
d) French
e) drama

Your school books are . . .

a) covered in paisley-print fabric
b) a bit muddy
c) filled with doodles
d) neat, tidy and full of good grades
e) rarely handed in on time